Ellis Peters is the pseudonym of Edith Pargeter, the distinguished author of many historical novels, including the *Heaven Tree Trilogy* and *The Marriage of Meggotta*. As Ellis Peters she also writes the bestselling Brother Cadfael mysteries. She lives in Shropshire.

ELLIS PETERS

The House of Green Turf

WARNER FUTURA

A *Warner Futura* Book

First published in Great Britain in 1969 by Collins
This edition published in 1992 by Warner Futura

Copyright © 1969 Ellis Peters

The right of Ellis Peters to be identified as author
of this work has been asserted by her in accordance
with the Copyright, Designs and Patents Act 1988.

ISBN 0 7088 5425 7

Printed and bound in Great Britain by
BPCC Hazells Ltd
Member of BPCC Ltd

Warner Futura
A Division of
Little, Brown and Company (UK) Limited
165 Great Dover Street
London SE1 4YA

CHAPTER I

BUT FOR A five-minute shower of rain, and a spattering of pennystone clay dropped from the tailboard of a lorry, Maggie Tressider would have driven on safely to her destination, that day in August, and there would never have been anything to cause her to look back over her shoulder and out of her ivory tower, nothing to make the mirror crack from side to side, nothing to bring any unforeseen and incomprehensible curse down upon her. She would have been in Liverpool by tea-time, relaxing before her concert; and then she would have dressed carefully and driven with her accompanist to the Philharmonic Hall, to give her usual meticulous performance in Brahms's "Alto Rhapsody," which was one of the things she did best, and Schumann's "*Frauenliebe und Leben*," which in her opinion was not. And the next day she would have shared the driving with Tom Lowell again on the way home, and then settled down to consider her next engagement, which was a recording session in London for a new and expensive *Fidelio*. And everything would have gone on hopefully and auspiciously, just as it had during all the past ten years, every new undertaking adding a further burnish to her reputation and fresh laurels to her crown.

But the clay fell, shaken loose from a careless load just where the road leaned the wrong way on the long curve by the brickworks; and a following lorry squashed the glutinous lump into a long, murderous slide, unobtrusive on the pale surface. And then the thin little shower came and passed, too feeble to wet the road thoroughly, but enough to leave sweaty globules all along the slide of clay, and give it a more treacherous sliminess. The trap was now all ready for the prey.

Maggie, new to the road but a good driver, estimated the angle of the curve as she reached it. It uncoiled right-handed in a sharp descent, one of those hazards due to be ironed out some day, when county funds permitted. It went on and on until it seemed they must be spiralling back beneath their own tracks, but Maggie continued to drive confidently round its convolutions, and checked her speed only slightly. At the most acute point of the curve the slide of clay waited for them, just where the gradient sagged away outwards instead of giving them support.

They hit it at forty, and everything went mad. Away went their wheels sidelong in a long glissade, while Maggie did all the correct things to adjust to the skid and get control again, and nothing responded. She fought the car with every sense and every nerve she had, and still inexorably, greasily, derisively, it went its own pig-headed way, outwards towards the white kerbing and the fall of tousled grass beyond. They hit the kerb and leaped shuddering into the air, and she dragged frantically at the wheel to get them back on to the road before they touched again, but then they were over, lurching in crazy, lunging bumps like an elephant amuck, down the tufted grass towards the quickset hedge below, and the stumps of three long-felled trees.

Earth and sky flickered and changed places, and sizzled and blinked out like broken film. She heard Tom cry out, and felt his hand beside hers on the wheel, which was no help at all. Doggedly she clung and swung, correcting headlong lurches as best she could, struggling to hold the car upright and bring it to a halt, but the gradient was against her. You might as well try to pat a bullet out of its course with your palm. But she never let go, and she never stopped trying.

She remembered yelling at Tom to loose his safety belt and jump, while they were still on the grass. But because of course he wouldn't, she remembered leaning across him and trying to open his door. A mistake, she had to take one hand from the wheel. Cool air blew in on her. The weight of the door swinging brought the car round and almost broadsided it short of the hedge, but its own impetus rolled it against the weight and sent it hurtling over in a slow somersault. The door flapped, like a wing trying to lift them clear, but as helpless as she was to save them. Then the seat beside her was empty, and the spiky shapes of the hedge surged upwards one moment, downward the next, to spear her, and the squat, solid, moss-grown stump of a tree launched itself from the sky to stamp her into the ground.

The world exploded in her face, and a fragmentation bomb in her lap. And then there was darkness, aeon upon aeon of darkness, and the last thing she knew, extended diminuendo long after everything else was gone, was her own voice, or perhaps only the silent phantom of her own voice, lamenting inconsolably: My God, what have I done! I've killed poor Tom! My God, what have I done, I've killed Tom, I've killed him . . . killed him . . . killed him . . .

*

Two voices were discussing her over her head. They didn't know that dead people can hear. Quite dispassionate voices, cool, leisurely, and low. Either they had no bodies, or dead people can't see. She was dangling just below the level of consciousness, clinging to the surface like the air-breathing nymph of some water creature.

"Beautiful, too!" said the first voice critically.

"Nobody's beautiful on the operating table," said the second voice cynically.

"Beautiful, gifted and famous. It seems some people *can* have everything."

"Except immortality."

"What *are* her chances?"

"Oh, pretty good now. Nothing's ever certain, but . . . pretty good. She had us on the run, though! Set on dying, you'd have said."

"Scale tipped the right way in the end. Pity if she'd slipped through our fingers. Maggie Tressider . . . what a loss!"

" '*Maggie is dead. And music dies!*' "

"Pardon?" said the first voice blankly, not recognising

Byrd's despairing tribute to Tallis, his master and idol. But
Maggie recognised it, and was enchanted, disarmed,
humbled.

"Never mind," said the second voice. "She'll do now.
That's one of us with the chance to begin again. I could
almost envy her.

Something pricked her thigh. She went down again grate-
fully, fathoms deep into the dark.

*

Faces loomed, receded and vanished like puffs of smoke.
Voices, some of them real and some illusory, whispered,
barked, shouted, fired themselves like pistol shots from every
corner of unreality, in the crazy round-dance of disorienta-
tion. Hands lifted her, trickles of water fed themselves into
her mouth. There were periods of light and sense, but she
always lost them again before she could orientate herself or
make anyone understand her. Pain, never acute but never
absent, ebbed and flowed in a capricious tide. Through a
shadowy underworld spiky with quickset hedges and shattering glass she pursued and was pursued, at every lucid
moment reaching out feverishly after whoever was nearest:
"Tom . . . please, find Tom! Never mind me, look for
Tom . . . he's hurt . . ." And all the while the dead man
pressed hard on her heels, tapping at her shoulder; but the
voice that panted in her ear was always her own voice, thinly
wailing: My God, what have I done? I've killed him . . .
killed him . . .

Later she hurt all over, and that meant that there were
senses there, nerves that were working, muscles that didn't
want to work; and she tried to move, and did move, and
that hurt more, but nevertheless was not discouraging.

A face hovered, impressed: "My, you're mobile!"

"Tom . . ." she said urgently. "Please, I've got to know
about Tom. . . ."

"Tom? Who's Tom?"

"Tom Lowell. He was with me in the car . . ."

"Oh, *he*'s all right. Don't worry about him. He was the

lucky one, he got off with only a few bramble scratches and mild concussion. He was discharged yesterday."

She couldn't believe it. "You mean he isn't dead? Really he isn't? You're not just trying to keep me quiet by telling me that?"

"Not a bit of it! He's far from dead. If you're fit for visits to-morrow he's coming in, so you can see for yourself. Got his face scratched, but that's all the damage you'll see. He was thrown out just short of the hedge. *You*'re the one who took the brunt, and you're going to be all right, too. Drink?"

"We were going to Liverpool," said Maggie, groping after departed urgencies that might have validity again any moment. "We should have been at a concert. . . ."

"Mr. Lowell fixed that as soon as he came round. We telephoned them, and they got somebody else. Everything's taken care of."

So there seemed nothing more to ask about, and nothing more to say. She sank back into a chaos now less frightening because almost meaningless. Everything was taken care of. Tom wasn't dead. After all, she would never have to face his wife and try to excuse herself for the crash that killed him. He was alive, not even badly hurt.

Then if it wasn't Tom, who was it, tapping her on the shoulder, treading on her heels, dunning her for his life?

It wasn't any delusion, he was still there; even in the instant of absolute relief over Tom he had still been there, close and faceless, making use of her voice because he had no voice of his own, being dead: My God, what have I done? He's dead, and I killed him! *My God, what have you done to me? Killed me . . . killed me . . . killed me . . .*

How could she have mistaken him for Tom? Only out of the remote past, where so much was forgotten, could something so ominous and shapeless surface again to haunt and accuse. When the waters are troublel, dead people rise. But all her dead were decently buried, and she had never done them any wrong.

"Nurse! There wasn't anyone else, was there? We didn't hit somebody else, when we crashed . . .?"

"There was nobody else around. Just the two of you, as if that wasn't enough! What are you worrying about? You're both going to be all right."

No answer there, either. Much longer ago, much farther away, than the badly-engineered curve by the brickworks. Somewhere, at some time, she had done something terrible to someone, something that destroyed him. Oh God, what was it? How could she know she had done it, and not know what it was? The silence that had covered it could only be her silence. She must have known at some time, and held her tongue in the hope of universal silence. And gradually drawn breath easily again, because there'd been no sound, nobody to rise up and accuse her, nobody to dig up what was dead, nobody she need fear, after all. Only herself, lulled, bemused, bribed, persuaded, subdued into acquiescence, but never convinced. Only herself and this roused ghost clawing at her shoulder, and this now constant and inconsolable ache inside her of a debt unpaid and unpayable.

*

"Well, how are you feeling this morning?" asked the ward sister, coming in on her daily round.

"Much better, thank you." The patient was pale, lucid and astonished among her pillows, staring great-eyed at a recovered world in which she seemed to find nothing familiar. "I'm afraid I've been causing you all a great deal of trouble."

"You haven't done so badly, considering. You did give them rather a run for their money in the theatre—very naughty reactions to the anaesthetic. But that's all over now. Your temperature's been down to normal since last night, and Nurse tells me you're eating well this morning. Keep it up, and we'll be getting you out of bed in a couple of days."

"I seem to have been lucky," said Maggie, flexing her legs experimentally under the bedclothes. "Everything works. What exactly did I do to myself?"

"It wasn't half as bad as it looked when they brought you

in. A lot of blood, but no breakages. But you were pretty badly cut about, down below, you're going to look like a Victorian sampler when you get all that plaster off. Never mind, the scars won't be where they show, and if you usually heal well you may not have much to show for it in a year or so. There've been any amount of callers enquiring after you. Your sister telephoned, and your brother . . . your agent . . . In a few days we'll let you have a telephone in here, but not just yet. But I think we could allow you visitors this afternoon. Mr. Lowell sent you the roses, and said he'd be in to see you the minute we let him."

"Wasn't I in a ward? I thought . . . I seem to remember more beds . . . a big room and a lot of people sleeping . . ."

"Your agent asked us to move you into a private room, as soon as he knew what had happened."

"Oh," said Maggie, "I see!" He would, of course, to him it would be a matter of first importance. "It sounds silly, but I don't even know what hospital this is. I'd never driven that road before."

"You're in the Royal, in Comerbourne. We're the nearest general to that nasty bend where you crashed. You're not the first we've had brought in from there, and I doubt you won't be the last. Take things easily, and don't worry about anything now, you're doing very nicely."

"Everybody's being very kind. I'm sorry to be a nuisance."

"It's what we're here for." The ward sister looked back from the doorway, and saw the dilated blue-black eyes following her steadily from the pillow, but without any real awareness of her. They gave her the curious impression that they were staring inward rather than outward. "There isn't anything troubling you, is there? If there's anything you want, anythng we can do for you, you've got a bell there by your bed."

"Thank you, really there's nothing more you can do for me."

*

There was nothing more any of them could do for her.

Not the ward sister, not the wiry little staff nurse with a bibful of pins, not the tall, splay-footed Jamaican beginner from Port Royal, who herring-boned up the ward like a skier climbing back up a slope, and warmed the air with her split-melon smile and huge, gay, innocent eyes; not the young houseman who made the daily rounds, nor the consultant surgeon who had sewn her torn thighs back into shape, not the anaesthetist who had kept her breathing on the table when it seemed she had been set on giving up the struggle. Nor her visitors, who came with flowers and chocolates as soon as they were allowed in: Tom Lowell, tongue-tied with unwary joy at seeing her on her way back to life, and half-inclined to blame himself, though heaven knew why, for what had happened; her agent, swooping in from London laden with roses and reassurances; a young conductor passing through Comerbourne on his way to an engagement in Chester; a famous tenor who had recorded with her a few months ago; a concert violinist, and others who had shared platforms with her. They sat by her bed for an hour or so, happy and relieved to find her recognisable for the same Maggie, with a steady pulse, a satisfactory blood pressure, and a voice unimpaired. They went away with the comfortable feeling of having visited and consoled the not-too-sick. There was nothing more she could do for them, or they for her.

The unidentified visitor, the one without a face, did not so much return after their going as sit with her silently throughout their stay, patient and apart, and move in to her heart's centre when they went away. Often, then, she turned her whole attention upon him suddenly, in the effort to startle him into revealing some feature by which he could be recognised, before the concealing mists swirled over him and hid everything; but he was always too quick for her. She would not give up the search, and he would not be found.

But the visitors went away content, finding her as they had always known her, even though she would never be the same again. True, she had survived, physically she was intact, now that she was over the unexpected hazard of the anaesthetic. We shall not all die, but we shall all be changed, she thought, left alone in the relaxed hour before supper. In a moment, in the twinkling of an eye. About as long as it takes for a somersaulting car to smash itself against a tree-stump, and spill you out among the broken glass and twisted metal on to the grass. And probably about as long as it takes to launch the decisive word or act that looks almost excusable at the moment, and only afterwards, long, long afterwards, turns out to have been your damnation.

*

She awoke from an uneasy sleep in mid-afternoon, to find a small, elderly, shaggy man in a white coat sitting beside her bed. She had seen him making his official rounds twice since her admission, and she knew he was the consultant surgeon who had perseveringly stitched Humpty-Dumpty together again; but until this moment she had never seen him still, and never without his retinue.

"Good!" he said. "I've been waiting for the chance to talk to you. You worry me."

"Do I? I'm sorry!" she said, startled, and her memory fitted one detail, at least, into its true place. "I know you now," she said obscurely, "you're the one who said I had a chance to begin again."

"Did I? I don't remember that. But you have, that's true enough. What are you going to do with it?"

"Use it, I hope."

"I hope so, too, but I'm not so sure of it as I was three days ago. You're my investment, I want to see you thriving. After a tricky start you got over your physical troubles marvellously, and believe me, you can think yourself lucky to have a constitution like yours. Your pulse is steady, your blood pressure's satisfactory, and your body's functioning like a first-class machine. But Sister tells me you've lost some weight and are losing your appetite. Why? Why have

you less energy than you had two or three days ago? Why
do you have nothing to say to anyone unless you're obliged
by politeness? And never use that telephone we gave you?"

Her eyes, which were the darkest, deepest blue he had
ever seen, and in any but this lofty light might have seemed
black, widened in alarm, astonishment and compunction.
"I didn't realise that," she said. "I'm sorry!"

"And for all this, let me tell you, there isn't the slightest
physiological reason. Your body's doing its job. Doing
everything it can to get well. So since there has to be a
reason why you've come to a halt, and even begun to lose
ground, the reason must be in your mind. Now probably
you'll tell me that what's in your mind is no concern of
mine," he said dryly, "but at least don't tell me there's
nothing damaging there, because I shan't believe you."

"No," said Maggie, and raised herself strenuously on her
pillow to be eye to eye with him. "No, I do realise . . . It
was you who put me together again." He understood what
she meant; it gave him rights in her. Every artist, every
craftsman, has the right to demand that his work shall not
be wasted by somebody else's wanton irresponsibility. "I
do want to get well," she said. "I want to go on singing—
what's the good of me, otherwise? And I want to do you
credit, too. It's a priority bill that I must pay before I can
get any peace. But, my God, don't you think I've been
trying?"

"I know you have. Even successfully, until something
else distracted your attention. Something with a higher
priority?"

She let her head fall back on the pillow. Her eyes closed
for a moment, but opened unwaveringly to hold him off.
There were defences there only an old man with privileges
could hope to breach, and even he only when the wind and
the hour and the mood were favourable. She was a strong,
fit woman, thirty-one years old and one of the treasures of
the world, even if she herself didn't know it, and he was
disposed to believe that she did; and unless somebody
managed to goad her back into living, she would draw in

upon herself and die of absent-mindedness. Literally absent-mindedness, for all her energy and will-power and passion were engaged elsewhere, and her body, however robust and heroic, could not survive unaided.

"No, don't say anything yet. Listen to me. I know you love what you do. I know you realise what you possess, a voice in a million. You couldn't use it as you do, if you didn't know its value. I'm your surgeon, it's in my own interests to ensure that what I do isn't erased by some other force, whether outside or inside my own province. But I'm a man, too, dependent upon music to a degree you maybe don't suspect. Would you be surprised to hear that I have every recording Maggie Tressider has ever made? You live by my grace, I live by yours. And I need you, I need you whole and effective, I need you because you excel, and your excellence belongs to me, as it does to everyone who feels and understands it. If you can use me, use me. I'm here to be used. It may not be surgery, but it comes somewhere within the bounds of healing, and that's my business. And this is a kind of confessional, too. I'm here to forget and be forgotten, afterwards."

She lay silent and motionless for a long time, her blue, unblinking stare wide and wary upon his face.

"You'd have to have faith in me, too," she said warningly, "or you'll take the easy way out and think I'm a mental case." Her voice, used now like a weapon, had recovered much of its resplendent viola tone; he had never heard anyone sound saner.

"*I'm being haunted,*" she said, "*by somebody I've killed.* A higher priority . . . that's what you said, isn't it? That's exactly my case. I'm possessed. I owe you and everyone here a return on your investment, I owe the world whatever it is I contribute. But I owe this ghost of mine a life. You can't get ahead of that, can you? I'm very much afraid my debts to you are going to be difficult to pay. By the time he's paid I shall be bankrupt."

The dark-blue gaze speared him suddenly, and found him appalled and pitying, exactly as she had suspected.

"I told you you'd think I was mad. It's all right, I quite understand. Sometimes I think so, too. That's when I lose ground. But if you really want me," she said, "you'd better believe me sane and go on listening. You did say this was a confessional, remember?"

"I remember. What you say now remains unsaid. Absolutely and eternally. And I believe it."

"I've done something terrible," said Maggie. "I don't even know what it is, or when it happened, but I drove somebody to his death. I knew it when I came round in the night, after the accident. He was there breathing down my neck, whispering to me that I'd killed him. Not at all vague or distant, absolutely real and present, but when I turn round to look for the details there's nothing to be found. Just this sense of guilt. What I feel is that somewhere, at some time, I failed somebody, or betrayed somebody . . . something unforgivable . . . Criminal? I don't know, I think it may have been, if only in keeping silent about something I knew. Somebody relied on me, and I turned my back and let him fall. What matters," she said, her eyes straining upwards into the quivering blue and white radiance of reflected light on the ceiling over her head, "is that he's dead, and I killed him."

She waited, almost disdainfully prepared for the soft, humouring tones that medical men keep for the mentally unstable.

"And have you managed," he asked, very soberly and thoughtfully, "to find anything in your memory that lends colour to this belief?"

"No. I've tried and tried, and I can't trace any such incident. But it's still there. He never stops treading on my heels."

"But there's no known ground for this obsession. Don't forget, you've been through fairly drastic surgery, and a considerable degree of shock. It isn't at all unusual for the kind of experience you've lived through to leave a nightmare residue, that may surface at the least expected moment. Details submerge, and a sense of horror remains, something you can't pin down. Something that passes gradually, if you concentrate on the live world and let it pass."

"No," she said instantly and chillingly. "You forget, it's almost a week now, and I've waited and held my breath, and it doesn't pass. Because it's real, not a dream at all, not a floating residue left to surface by chance. *It's there!* In the corner of my eye always, and when I turn to look at it, it's everywhere but where I'm looking. I don't know when, I don't know how, but it's something I did, and I can't get away from it."

"You do realise, don't you, that even if there is some factual basis for it, it may turn out to be in some incident grotesquely out of proportion to the feeling you have about it?"

"It may," she agreed; but he knew by the set of her face that she did not believe in that possibility.

"But even so, if it does exist in your past, however inadequately, then it must be possible to run it to earth."

"That's what I've been trying to do for days. I've been forwards and backwards through my life, poking under all the stones I can find. At first I took it for granted it was Tom, you see . . . that I'd killed him when I crashed the car. But they told me at once that he was safe. Then I thought that there might have been somebody else involved in the accident, but there wasn't. It isn't as simple as that, and it isn't as recent. The knowledge seemed to come from very deep, as if an earthquake had split the ground and thrown up something from miles down. There are no levels any more, everything's torn up and thrown about, and everything has to settle all over again afterwards, and make a new surface to walk on. The first steps are liable to be pretty shaky. And buried things may break out and meet you in the way."

He saw the quickened breathing heaving her breast, and the hectic flush of exertion flicking her cheekbones. "I'm tiring you," he said.

"No, don't go! No, you're helping me. After I'd dredged up every recollection I could, right back to school, I did try, you see, to put it out of my mind. I told myself it was one of those freaks, the shock and the fright and the pain choosing to hit me after the event in this way. Nothing behind it. But I couldn't satisfy myself, and I'm afraid you won't be able to satisfy me, either. I'm not running a temperature, I'm not in shock, I haven't any worries, my career will wait for me the short time it has to wait, and all I have to do is lie around and enjoy myself while I get well. There simply is no reason at all—is there?—why this terrible conviction of guilt should stay with me still. Only one possible reason. That it's true, that it's justified."

"But if there existed any real source for it, you would have found it." It did not convince him, and he knew as soon as it was out that it would not convince her.

"No, because I'm the wrong person to do the searching. Oh, I *believe* I want to find it, but how can I be *sure*? Isn't it possible that there's at least as much of me trying to stamp it back into the ground, quickly, before I ever get a good look at it? Isn't that the most likely reason why I always see it out of the corner of my eye?"

"But did you never stop to consider that you have relatives, associates, friends, people who have been intimately involved in your life for years, and none of them accuses you of anything? Do you really believe you've committed some mortal fault against another person, without a single one of your acquaintances knowing anything about it? Is there an empty place anywhere in your life where you even *could* have done this hypothetical thing, in absolute isolation from any witness? That would rule out anything but the cruder possibilities, like flat, planned murder, that *has* to be kept secret. And that would involve more complications, like skills I very much doubt if you possess." He span out his theme to its ultimate absurdity. "And a body. And there never was a body featuring in your affairs, I take it?"

"No . . . no body." She shivered, and passed the heel of her hand over her eyelids. "It wouldn't be like that. There are more oblique ways of killing. Even without meaning to. But you see, it's just because I've been dead in a way myself that I *must know*. After coming back to life again as I have, I've got to make this a new beginning, otherwise it will be unbearable. If I have something shameful buried somewhere in my past, then I want to know what it is. I want to settle the account, if it can be settled. I want to be out of debt."

"And you've said nothing of all this to anyone else? To your agent, or your family?"

The look she gave him, beginning with blank incomprehension and burning up into horrified recoil, more than answered that question. Clearly it would have been unthinkable to confide in any one of those circling satellites. She had dealt openly with him only because of his reassuring distance from her, and because he was a professional with a legitimate and impersonal interest in her recovery. And only a moment ago he had come very close to touching her hand, by way of establishing a closer contact! If he had done it he would have lost her irrecoverably.

"Well, supposing now," he said carefully, "that someone else, someone completely detached, took over this search for you?"

He grudged her to the psychiatrists, but they might well be the obvious answer, if she could be persuaded to co-operate. And Harlingford was a good man, and old enough to see her with a disenchanted eye. If, he hedged wryly, any man still living is old enough for that. To love her would be to be powerless to help her, that was clear, for at the first touch, no more than the meeting of eyes, she would draw back out of reach, retreat into the castle and bar the doors. Now I wonder, he thought, I really wonder why?

"Supposing someone else, someone who makes a job of that kind of thing, took over the stone-turning for you? If he found some lost detail—most probably perfectly innocent—to account for the setting up of this cancer in your mind, would that satisfy you? You would have to have faith in your man, of course. But there are people, you know, who are trained in these techniques, highly skilled professionals who take this sort of thing as their special field."

If he had only known it, he had gone about this oblique approach all too gently; they were on different wavelengths, and communication as he understood it had ceased, though to her mind he had just begun to make sharp and practical sense. She sat up alertly. The word professional had a reassuring sound in her ears. Why not? He was right, what she needed was someone who knew how to set about unearthing lost incidents, someone who put his talents on the market at a fair price, and could be hired to do a specific job on a business footing. In a relationship like that, mutually agreed, there would be no violation of privacy.

"Would you like me to put your case in the hands of somebody like that, and leave it to him to do your searching for you? And if the expert fails to turn up anything discreditable, then will you be satisfied?"

"Yes," she said eagerly, "oh, *yes*! That's what I need, somebody completely objective. But I shouldn't know where to look for the right person, and I don't want to ask anyone else to . . . to be an intermediary for me. Find me a good private detective, and I'll turn the whole nightmare over to him, and abide by whatever he finds."

CHAPTER II

His NAME was Francis Killian, and he was forty-one years old. Strictly speaking, he was not what is usually thought of as a private detective at all, and he never called himself one. The small plate on his office door above the book-shop in Market Street, Comerbourne, said only: "Confidential Enquiries," and that was precisely what he dealt in. He didn't touch divorce business or commercial spying; sometimes he wondered why, since he had no very inflated opinion of his own holiness, and there was more money in these lines than in the cold, retired researches he did undertake. An eventful life, which had begun its adulthood with national service in Korea, could hardly leave him many illusions; and even after that unspeakably horrible trap had opened and released him, scarred for life, he had half-chosen and half-drifted into situations and callings which were not for the squeamish. Trying, perhaps, to rediscover disgust as the clean feel it, a luxury out of reach of those already soiled.

So he couldn't congratulate himself that it was any particular moral purity that had won him a recommendation from one of Comerbourne's most respectable solicitors to one of Comerbourne's most eminent surgeons, improbably in quest of a private enquiry agent "for a friend," of course! All that had kept Francis acceptable to such clients was a fastidious sense of cleanliness, a cold dislike of the feel of dirt. If he still had moral scruples, it was from old habit, and they were by no means clearly defined.

He was unmarried and alone. He hadn't always been alone. He remembered women he had known, too many of them and too intimately, but all past. He expected now to continue alone. You can stand only so much self-exposure and so much self-division; in his case very little, the godhead in him was a jealous god. It had been clear to him now for five years that there must be no more women gnawing away at the edges of his integrity. Such as it was! Not the world's treasure, that was certain; but all the treasure he had and he valued it.

So Francis Killian was a lonely man, in the large sense that precludes any feeling of grievance in being alone. And he worked hard, as men alone do, in dry, precise, painstaking ways that commended him chiefly to the legal profession. Most of his work was done for solicitors, tracing witnesses to accidents, combing ancient church registers, making abstracts of tedious documents; and for scholars and writers, running to earth elusive authorities, compiling précis of acts and regulations, searching records for lost details Sometimes he traced lost persons, too, and even lost ancestries, some of them better lost for good. Occasionally he consented to undertake a shadowing job, where a witness was liable to abscond, or worried parents wished to keep a wary eye on a young son's questionable associates.

Dealing with documents was clean, sterile, congenial business that neither moved nor disturbed him, and that was what counted. It brought him in a modest living, and in money for its own sake he had no great interest. Indeed he had reached a midway breathing-space in his life when he had only a detached interest in anything, and what mattered most to him was to have the ground about him cleared of all encumbering passions and all human entanglements, like a man who finds it necessary to throw away all his possessions in order to feel free.

There were still things in the world, however, that gave him positive, profound, irresistible pleasure, burdening him with a kind of obligation to look again at a human race which could occasionally produce perfection. The first and greatest of these unwilling relationships he had was with music. Against the grain he conceded that there must still be hope for a species which had produced Mozart.

So against his instincts he agreed to consider stepping out of character to oblige Maggie Tressider. He thought of her as a voice rather than a woman, but the voice needed a human vehicle, and according to the old man the vehicle, the superb mechanism that produced that inimitable sound, was seriously threatened. Her recovery, he said, was being impeded by an obsession.

Any other name, and Francis Killian would have astonished and affronted his visitor by saying no. Obsessions were not in his line.

The old man wasn't enjoying his errand. He would much rather have handed her over to the head-shrinkers, of course, and kept it, as it were, in the family. He had entered the office stepping with the delicacy of a duchess slumming, and been curiously disarmed, even reassured, by the pale, austere, orderly room, as clinical in its way as his own consulting-room. He too could appreciate professionalism. But the man behind the desk had cancelled out the soothing effect of his own environment. There would always be something ambivalent about Francis, however gravely he comported himself, a faint aura of self-caricature, as if in despising mankind he could never completely conceal his despite against himself.

If Gilbert Rice could have retreated then, he would have done it; but Rattray, Rattray, Bell and Rattray—all four of them—had testified that this man was secret, reliable and conscientious, and to open the case to yet another operative was unthinkable. And Francis redeemed himself. At the mention of Maggie's name he froze, abandoning whatever he had been about to say, and sat thinking for a long minute, honestly eye to eye with his visitor. Then he said: "Tell me about it. If I can help Miss Tressider, I will."

"You understand, it is she who insists on employing a private detective. I . . . it was a misunderstanding. I would have preferred to recommend a psychiatrist. But Miss Tressider is a strong-willed woman, and very clear about her own state of mind. Whether it is a psychiatrist or a detective she needs, the fact remains that she can only be helped with her own co-operation, and she absolutely refuses a psychiatrist."

Francis readjusted his image of her at once; she might, indeed, be rejecting what she most needed, but a woman who knew her own mind so firmly might well be a reliable witness. His own instinct, had anyone proposed to meddle with his mind, would have been to defend his flawed privacy to the death. The unknown woman who was Orpheus, who was Eboli, who was disembodied beauty shut in a body by some cosmic paradox, moved a step nearer to him.

"And you think," said Francis shrewdly, "that the first step in curing her is to act as if you're taking her preoccupation seriously. In short, I shall be fulfilling my only useful function by going through the motions of trying to trace the thing that's worrying her. In that case, the answer is no. If I enter her employ I shall do my best for her, and it's from her I shall take my orders. If she wants me to look for a skeleton in her cupboard, I shall look for it. I may even find it But I can't be hired to jolly her along towards recovery by *pretending* to look for it. *You* don't believe," he said curiously, "that there's really anything to be found, do you?"

After a struggle with his distaste and distrust, Gilbert Rice surprised him. "Yes," he said flatly, "there is something. Almost certainly something. I'll be quite open with you, Mr. Killian. In my judgment Miss Tressider is a person of quite exceptional generosity and integrity, who has fared rather badly in her personal relationships. She comes from a very ordinary lower-middle-class family—you understand, I am using current terms simply because they are useful in establishing a picture—whose other members have sponged on her from the beginning of her celebrity without shame and without gratitude, and privately resent her pre-eminence as much as they publicly rejoice in it. I believe she has behaved towards all her relatives and associates with great loyalty, which in her heart she knows very well is cast on stony ground. I think it is entirely possible that once, just once, she rebelled and recoiled, that just once she turned and tore somebody, in a protest which was overdue. I suppose it's even possible that there was a disastrous result, for someone who surely deserves little sympathy. She is incapable of real malice or meanness. But her standards are high. I think from her point of view there may well be something to regret. I believe it would be better if she knew what it was, and could be forced to accept it. You need not be afraid of the result, if you do run the thing to earth. She has a sense of responsibility to the rest of us, too. Whatever you find, you won't destroy her, you can only liberate her. She knows of what a marvel she is the custodian."

Fantastic, Francis thought, shaken clean out of his objectivity. This antique pillar of society, thirty years established, father and grandfather, suddenly wrenching his heart open over a neurotic young woman he never saw before, because some accident of nature gave her the voice of an archangel. And how if he's right? How if she really needs to be rid of an incubus that might kill her? No more

immortal Orpheus, only that lament on a gramophone
record, slowly paling for want of new, living breath. Stiff
little, grey little stuffed shirt as he might be, Maggie Tressider's surgeon had the courage of his convictions.

"I take it," said Francis carefully, drawing the classic pro-
file of Orpheus on the half-filled page of notes before him,
"that the best thing I can do is come and talk to Miss Tressider during ordinary visiting hours. . . . This evening?"

He went home and played the Gluck records. She was
better even than he remembered her. It was not a dark,
weighty, velvet contralto, but agile, thrilling and true, a
quality in it that sheared through the heart like pure pain,
like love itself, excising everything of lesser urgency. It was
the voice the old man was in love with, of course. No face
could live up to it, much less the heart and the being that
went with the face.

She had a crooked mouth in photographs, and a wide,
defensive glance, like a child's, and a more than usually
asymmetrical face, larger on the right side.

Well, there was the voice to be saved.

*

She was sitting up in bed when he came, looking exactly
like all those other women in the long ward next door, pol-
ished and brushed and neatly tucked in for visiting-time.
She had even the same half-apprehensive, half-expectant
look as they had, and her eyes, like theirs, enlarged in a face
blanched and honed to transparency by the experience of
suffering, turned towards the doorway of her room as soon
as his hand touched the handle, and transfixed him as he
entered with their blue intensity. She looked glad, and
eager, and afraid; exactly as if he had really been a personal
visitor, and one to whom she had long looked forward.

"Miss Tressider? My name is Killian."

"It's very good of you," she said, "to come so promptly."
Her speaking voice was low-pitched, warm and vibrant.
"Please sit down. I believe Mr. Rice has explained to you
what's worrying me? . . . what I want you to find out for
me?"

It seemed that everything was to be conducted with despatch, practically, as between business associates, without any suggestion of anguish. Unless, he thought a moment later, you looked too closely at the fine-drawn lines of her face, which had still something of the chill of shock about them, the faint, reflected image of death as it missed its hold on her; or deeply enough into the wide, wild stare of the eyes to discover the fixed, silvery gleam of panic behind their honest, well-mannered blueness. She shopped for the commodity she needed with the directness of a child, but there was nothing childish about her need.

It was illuminating, too, that the paperbacks he had brought with him came as a shock to her, and an embarrassment. When he laid them on the bed convenient to her hand she touched them blankly, and didn't know what to do or say. The thanks came mechanically, and what was really on her mind couldn't find words. How right he had been to pass up roses! Unless, of course, he wanted her to withdraw the offer of this job? He still wasn't clear about that, but if he had wanted it, roses would have been as good a way as any of making sure. He wasn't here to have any personal relationship with her, she mustn't be touched. All that he must inevitably discover about her she would countenance and assist as case-notes necessary to the job, but never as the impalpable web of a man's understanding. This would have to be strictly clinical. So much the better; that suited Francis.

"It seemed advisable to be as convincing a visitor as possible," he said dryly, "and you'll have observed that they never come empty-handed. The women in the ward might not notice. The staff certainly would. I take it I'm right in thinking that *only* Mr. Rice is in your confidence?"

"Oh," she said, flushing, "I see! Yes, of course, that was thoughtful of you. I thought . . . I was rather afraid that you might be too well known to pass unnoticed, in any case."

"I'm hardly the celebrity type of detective," he assured her, amused and disarmed. "Few of us are, if the truth be told. Nobody here is likely to know who I am or what I do, and your privacy needn't be compromised."

"That's what I should prefer, if it's possible. But of course you must include the books and everything in your expenses."

The tone was perhaps a little arrogant, but so, in all probability, had his been.

"We can come to an agreement about all that later," he said. "Since our time's limited, what I think you should be doing now is lying back and relaxing, while you tell me yourself about this experience that made you send for me. By this time I take it you've found a way of surrendering yourself into the hands of doctors when you have to? Consider me one more in the same category. Close your eyes and shut me out if it makes it any easier. Most of us do that with doctors, when the handling begins."

"And dentists," said Maggie unexpectedly, and smiled.

"And dentists." It might, he conceded ruefully, be a better analogy. "I shall have to take notes. You won't mind that? They'll all be destroyed, afterwards."

"Yes, I understand." She let her head fall back on the pillow. "I want to do everything that may help you to find out . . . what it is that's haunting me. You understand, I must know. There'll be no peace for me, no possibility of living normally, unless I know. *He* wanted me to put it out of my mind, but I can't do that. If I've done somebody a terrible wrong, and now for the first time I *feel* what I've done how can I just push it away and pretend I know nothing about it? Then he wanted me to put myself in the hands of a psychiatrist. Why should I do that? I don't want it rationalised out of existence, if it really does exist, *I want it put right!* I'm sorry," she said, suddenly fixing those disturbing eyes upon his attentive face, "if you find all this a little unbalanced. All that got through to me was the fact of my guilt. It's because I can't give a rational account of the thing that I need you. Do *you* think I'm out of my wits?"

"No," he said, "I think you are very much in command of them. Tell me!"

She told him, slowly, carefully, picking her words with concentration and precision, like a party to a case in court who must make the right impression now or never. And after a few moments she closed her eyes and put him out of her recognition except as a disembodied confessor, the better to feel her way towards objectivity. It seemed that her passion for truth and justice was large enough to compel absolute candour, as if she felt herself to be addressing God. In his experience women could be devious even in their prayers, but he would have staked his reputation that this one was not.

Maggie talked and Francis listened, made notes, and watched her face, a pure oval, its irregularities hardly discoverable here in the flesh. Photographs always exaggerate any disproportion in the features; but her photographs were almost caricatures, so far were they from doing her justice. It was largely a matter of colouring. Those dark, dark eyes of hers you would have expected to be softly purple-black like a pansy, but instead they were the startling, piercing blue of high-altitude gentians, as vivid as noon in their midnight darkness. And now he came to think of it, that was exactly the colouring of her dark, dark voice, too. And her hair, refined English mouse-brown in pictures, who could have guessed it would be this unbelievable tint between dark gold and orange-russet, even subtly greenish in the shadows, the colour of the budding foliage of an oak tree in spring? She was much thinner than in any photograph he had ever seen of her; but then, she was probably much thinner now than she'd been a few weeks ago, after extensive surgery, and with this obsession eating her alive.

He made the same discovery as the anaesthetist had made, paying his midnight visit to her in the ward to make sure she had really decided to take up the business of breathing again. She was beautiful. Very beautiful. It seems some people *can* have everything. Except, of course, peace of mind and a quiet conscience.

It was at about this point that he observed the first interesting peculiarity about her narrative. He didn't make a note of it; it wasn't necessary.

"Thank you," he said when she fell silent. "That was very comprehensive, and I doubt if I have many questions to ask. If you'd had any clue to time and place you would have included it. But I gather we can't limit the possibilities at all, apart from ruling out the last few years. Forgetting is mortally easy, easier than remembering, but it does take a little time. Assuming this haunting has a foundation in fact, if it had been recent it would have surfaced more completely, with more detail."

"But is it genuinely possible," she asked, opening her eyes wide, "to forget something so important? Even after years?"

"It's possible, all right. What we retain over a lifetime is only an infinitesimally small proportion of the whole. Think how many impressions are run through in an hour, and how many brief acquaintances in a year. The most phenomenal memory can't contain a tenth of the total."

"But something like that . . . a matter of life and death . . . *that* would surely be retained, whatever was thrown out."

"We don't know that it was a matter of life and death, or that it seemed so important then. Maybe this is hindsight. I don't suggest your condition conjured up a totally illusory bogy, but I do think it possible that it magnified and distorted a comparatively innocuous incident. Wait," he said reasonably, "until you know."

"You forget," said Maggie mildly, "that I'd just slipped through death's fingers. When you find yourself staring at close range into judgment day, you get your values right."

"Not necessarily. Not unless you believe fear to be the best introduction to truth. Even the just aren't going to feel too sure of themselves on judgment day."

"Oh, no," said Maggie oddly, "I wasn't afraid. You go clean through that, you know. It doesn't apply any more. Even now it isn't like being afraid, it's just that it's impossible to live without *knowing*. Like Oedipus. There isn't any possibility of turning back and letting well alone. There wouldn't be any solid ground to stand on. And you can't sing without truth!"

No, *she* couldn't, he quite saw that. It took a bit of believing, in such a bogus world, but this woman had never severed her infant relationship with reality, and while she felt truth to be impaired everything would be devalued for her, even her art. He knew then that he was committed, not simply to accepting her commission, but to bringing it to a successful conclusion.

"We still have half an hour. If you're not too tired, I should like you to begin talking to me about yourself. Right from the beginning, your family, your childhood, things you remember. Names you remember. Don't worry about looking for the seeds of this present trouble. Forget about it now. It may come to light of itself, it won't if you try to trace it. Tell me who played with you, who were your friends, your fellow-students . . ." Though the name that mattered she might not even recognise; she was almost sure by now that she had excised it from her memory for good reason, and eternally, unless some act of God or of Francis Killian raised it again to confront her. Between the conflicting needs and wants of the divided halves of her, what was a man in her employ supposed to do?

But she couldn't sing without truth; she had said it, not he. And she couldn't live without singing.

"Just talk to yourself," he said, "and I'll be quiet."

And she talked, and he was very quiet. Her lips moved slowly and thoughtfully, unrolling before him a cartoon of that ordinary family of hers, odd little vignettes of her schooldays, without sentimentality, without nostalgia, almost without interest. She had had to leave her kin to find her kind, like many another. Not a matter of class at all, but of quality, which is a different and a mysterious thing. She mentioned names faithfully. Most he did not bother to note down, but some were still quick in her memory. He was sensitive to the intonations now. And then her first singing days, the little local successes, the audition that took her into

Doctor Paul Fredericks' classes, the serious study beginning. No doubt of the urgency now, his pen was busy writing down names that mattered to her almost as gravely as her own.

She was still twelve years back in time when the bell rang for the end of visiting-hour. She opened dazed eyes. Her forehead was moist, but the lines of her face were relaxed and tranquil.

"I'll come the day after to-morrow," he said, putting away his notebook, "in the evening, if you can manage to deflect all your other visitors. I've tired you out too much . . . I'm sorry!"

"Oh, no!" she said quickly. "I'm glad! Just to be doing something about it is worth anything. I feel happier now. I trust you."

Now that, he thought bitterly, winding his way across the car park to his third-hand Riley, is about the most unfair and terrifying thing one human being can say to another. She trusts me! To come up with miracles, to get her out of her little private hell. What sort of spot does that put me in? But of course, she'll be paying my daily rate and all expenses . . . even the paperbacks! That puts it on quite a different footing for her, all she's asking is fair work for fair pay. But what does it do for me? It may take more than a little patient research, more than leg work, more than you can buy for any daily retainer, to turn up X for her and get the thorn out of her flesh.

Still, he reflected, driving home to his flat in Market Street, bare as a hermitage, he had got one positive thing out of this first session. All the female names he had written down were recorded only as possible sources of information; apart from that he might as well cross them off at once. Maggie Tressider was quite certainly honest in claiming that she could not recapture a single limiting fact about the identity of X. But every time she spoke of her victim and persecutor she said "he."

*

He went to the trouble to check on her family, though he

felt and found that they were of no interest. Her parents were dead, the father long ago, while Maggie was still at school, the mother four years ago of heart disease. There remained a sister and a brother, Alec, both older than Maggie. The brother played the horn in a Midland orchestra, well enough to hold his place but not well enough ever to get any farther. A little probing produced a picture not at all unexpected; he had been trading on his sister's reputation and his relationship to her ever since she emerged into celebrity. He had made one flying visit to see her in the hospital, since it wasn't far out of his way. Rice was of the opinion that he had come for money, and hadn't gone away empty-handed, but he did at least make himself pleasant, affectionate and cheerful while he was there.

The married sister, eldest of the three, lived in Hertfordshire with an insurance-agent husband and two children. She hadn't visited. There was a record of telephone enquiries from her, beginning with an agitated lament on the first evening, before Maggie was up from the theatre, expressing endless devotion and the fixed intention of leaving everything and rushing to her bedside; but the tone had cooled off after it became clear that the bed was not going to be a death-bed. Mrs. Chalmers still called in with loving messages, but she didn't suggest coming. These details Francis also gleaned from Rice, who had them from the ward sister, through whom all those earlier phone calls had been channelled.

It began to seem as if all those who professed affection for her also harboured in secret a corrosive resentment. Yet everything went to show that she had remained loyal and generous to her family and early associates. Maybe that was her really unforgivable virtue. If she had shaken them off and gone her own way unimpeded, they could at least have felt that she was down on their human level, and taken pleasure in her flaws for their own comfort. People who have everything stir in ordinary mortals a venomous ambition to take everything from them, or if that's impossible, at least to spoil what is spoilable. No, Maggie had never caused any of her tribe to lament at her shoulder in the night. They were much more likely, given the chance, to ruin and despoil her.

Then there were the others, colleagues, fellow-singers, accompanists, conductors, admirers. Would-be lovers, most of them, whether they knew it or not, though a few had the integrity and detachment to be disinterested friends to her into the bargain. God knew she had need of those, they seemed to have been few and far between in her life. The music teacher at her local school, perhaps, who had first realised what a glorious instrument she possessed, and done his best to help her develop its possibilities. And afterwards, Paul Fredericks, that eccentric and wealthy old genius who had spent the last years of his life squandering the profits of his own musical career on the musicians of the future. But how many more?

Plenty of would-be lovers, though, from the modest admirers of her girlhood, through the teeming procession of her fellow-students, to the celebrities who surrounded her now. And wasn't there, somewhere in the sweet chorus of their devotion, a slightly sour note, too? The courting male knows his worth, and expects to make an impression, but Maggie Tressider had always stayed unattainable. They still praise and they still pursue, when the object of the pursuit is such a valuable cult image and status symbol; but after a while a slight acidity sets in, the heart goes out of the charade, and something alien comes to birth in its place. Spite?

He didn't realise, until he tapped at the door of her room for the second time, and saw her propped on her pillows with delicately made-up face and burnished hair to receive him, exactly what it was about her that disturbed him most. He entered with his memory marking off like spent beads the names of her adorers, who were legion; and there in the white bed in the white room, tense and still, sat this one slender, solitary creature, the cobalt mirrors of her eyes waiting for a human image to reflect, so that she could be peopled. He had never known anyone round whom such numbers of worshippers revolved; and he had never known anyone so intensely and disastrously alone.

*

She was a good client, patient and humble. She was ready to pick up her autobiography where she had left it two days before, and even paid him the compliment of following his recipe for relaxation while she recollected, as if he had indeed been one more doctor with authority over her, if only a temporary authority. Slack in her pillows, with closed eyes, she recorded her testimony; and in the pauses, which were frequent but brief, long enough for thought but not for concealment, he watched her marble stillness, even her breath held, and thought, what would happen if one kissed this Sleeping Beauty? Would she wake up? On the contrary, she would withdraw into the hundred-year-long death-sleep at the first touch. You'd be lucky if you didn't impale yourself on the thorns before you ever reached her mouth.

"Dr. Fredericks used to pick out a small group of his pupils every spring and autumn, and take them on a tour of the Continent. He had good connections everywhere there, and it was his way of giving us proper concert experience before we tackled the big things. Freddy's Circus, we all called it. We used to attend some of the smaller festivals, and fill in with concerts all through Switzerland and Austria, and part of Germany too. There'd be two or three solo singers, and maybe a couple of instrumentalists, usually a pianist—one of the accompanists was always good for a concerto or two —and maybe a violinist, and a small orchestra. It cost him the earth to keep it all up, but now and again he even made a profit. I went three times. Once in 1954, in the autumn. I was eighteen. And then both the tours in 1955. After that I had my first big break, I was asked to sing Cherubino. He let me take it, so I knew I was ready. I never went abroad with him again, there were concerts, engagements, recordings . . . things began to go very fast. Two years later, Freddy died. In Bregenz, at the festival. There weren't any more Circuses."

"And who was with you on those tours? Can you remember?"

She mentioned several names. Two of them had followed her aloft, though less rapidly. One had died in a plane crash. Some were still, and presumably for ever, lost in obscurity.

"I don't remember any others. Oh, yes, the last time there was a change, because Freddy's sister, who always used to tour with us and act as chaperone for the girls, had to go into hospital just before we left, and one of his old pupils came along with us instead. Bernarda Elliot was her concert name. I think it was her maiden name. She was a contralto . . . a good one, but she'd been married for quite a time then, to somebody named Felse. She was living somewhere in the West Midlands, I remember. She came along with us just to oblige Freddy, and only that once. It was the only tour Miss Fredericks missed. She died, too, only a few months after Freddy. Voluntarily, I think. You know what I mean? They'd always worked together, without him the world wasn't worth hanging on to."

"I know," said Francis. "This Cherubino . . . that was at Covent Garden, wasn't it?"

"Yes, I was lucky. We recorded with the same cast, afterwards. It wasn't the best 'Figaro' ever, but it got a lot of notice."

From then on it had been simply a climb from one eminence to another, steadily extending her range, always waiting for a few additional years to bring new works and maturer parts within her grasp. She told him about it just as she had experienced it, without either arrogance or modesty, and it dawned on him suddenly that she was not quite the gifted child he had begun to believe her, that this headlong simplicity and directness of hers was not a property of innocence, but the deliberate choice of an adult mind, the weapon of a woman with a great deal to do and only one lifetime in which to do it. Maggie Tressider had no time to waste on circumlocutions. There was, it seemed, at least one quality in her which might well destroy either her or anyone who got in her way. Generous, scrupulous, loyal, all these she might be, but ambitious she certainly was. Not for herself so much as for the voice of which she was the high priestess. If ever there was a clash of interests, she would sacrifice everything and everybody to that deity, including Maggie Tressider.

By the time the bell rang to send him away, she had arrived at the present. Iris-circled, with half-transparent lids veined like snowdrops, her eyes remained closed for a moment after she was silent. The long lashes that lay on her cheeks were coloured like her hair, green-bronze-gold. When they rolled back from the wide stare that fastened unerringly on his face, the unveiled blue of her eyes was blinding.

It was then that it happened to him, sharp and clean as a knife-thrust, so that for an hour afterwards he never felt the pain.

"I'll contact you," he said, "as soon as I have anything to report. It may be a few days, but I'll ring you."

"Yes . . ." She wanted to ask what was in his mind, whether he had got anything at all out of her self-examinings; but she refrained. She had said that she trusted him, and now it was in his hands. "I feel better," she said, offering him the one encouragement and commendation she had to give. "Since you came I haven't lost any more weight. And I *sleep* now. I'm going to get well."

"Of course!" he said.

"And to put this right . . ." She smiled at him, a grave, grateful, impersonal smile. The burden of her confidence sagged heavily on his heart, and deep within him, secretly and slowly, the mortal wound began to bleed.

*

It was half-way through the evening before the numbness thawed away, and the injustice and indignity and rage and pain, the reasoned hopelessness and irrational hope, all hit him together.

He was sitting over his notebook with a full ashtray at his elbow, methodically compiling lists of names and considering the significance of the periods into which her life fell. There was always more to be gained by sitting and thinking, and evaluating what was given, than by rushing about questioning people, and he had his starting point.

"I've done something awful to *him* . . . killed *him* . . ." '*He's* here with me all the time, *he* never leaves me . . ." "It wouldn't be so bad if I could ever see *him* clearly . . ." Where there's no precise identification the masculine pronoun can embrace the feminine, too, of course. Maybe! But that was by no means the effect of the repeated "he" in her mouth. She didn't know even the sex of her enemy; no, but some spark of her subconscious knew, all right. All Lombard Street to a china orange, X was a man.

What sort of man? Not a member of her family; those she bore with, visited occasionally, subsidised as a matter of course. Rice had suggested that there might have been some such hanger-on who chose the wrong moment, or the wrong approach, and started in her a spurt of distaste that caused her for once to lash out in rebellion against her rôle. But did any of them matter to her enough to make that probable? Francis thought not. And whoever provoked her into cruelty would have to matter to her pretty fundamentally.

The more he thought about it, the more clearly did X put on the likeness of the one person who was so conspicuously absent from Maggie's life. A face so rigidly excised from memory might well belong to the one man who wasn't there.

Plenty of men had loved Maggie, but not one of them, by her own account and the world's, had Maggie ever loved. Never once had she mentioned the word "love." And that in itself was remarkable enough to arrest attention. Here was a gifted, beautiful woman, still defensively alone at approaching thirty-two. On the face of it that was the most mysterious thing about her. Why did she never marry? Because she was married to her art? Even so, why did she never, apparently, even consider taking husband or lover, never let any of the candidates get within arm's-length of her? Take a step too near her, and she would take three away from you, and then keep retreating until she was out of sight. He had seen it for himself, and so, if he wasn't mistaken, had Gilbert Rice. So what was wrong with her? What was the block that shut men out? The same that blotted out the face of X?

And if the hunt for X was the hunt for the invisible, the non-existent lover, the only one who got past her guard, where was he most likely to be found? Somewhere fairly far back, or she could not have expunged him so completely and for so long. In the world's eye not, perhaps, a very great figure in her life, or, again, she could not have forgotten him so successfully; yet great enough in retrospect to turn her whole life barren afterwards. *What was it she had done to him?*

No need to look back as far as childhood or early adolescence, either, because this was a thing that had fixed its claws into her adult being, and pierced deep. Somewhere at the emergence of the woman, say at eighteen or nineteen, when her career suddenly opened before her and she knew she was going to be great, when she was intoxicated and dazzled by music, and men, perhaps, faded into the background just when they should have been growing clear and important. Twelve or thirteen years ago. In twelve years she had had time to suppress a lot of regrets, to forget genuinely a lot of once-important people.

He performed, almost idly, the small exercise of looking back twelve years in his own life. Where had he been then? More to the point, with whom? He found a narrow boat on a Midland canal, a summer frittered away on an antique business that had folded under him because he didn't work at it, and a woman who had been the reason for his lack of application; but when it came to recalling the woman, she was only a small, blank, woman-shaped space without face or name. Nothing but an empty shape and a bitter taste, and no guilt except the guilt he felt for the squandering of whatever promise he'd ever had, and that held no mystery.

And then, abruptly, like a flower bud opening marvel-

lously under the camera, the pale non-recollection put on
colour and form and life, the head flushed into the incredible colour of oak foliage in spring, the burning blue eyes
pierced him as they had pierced him an hour ago, and the
searing realisation of his position broke out like blood at
last, and he knew he was lost. Who had he thought he was,
writing off women so confidently? Who did she think she
was, writing off men?

For the first time in his life he hadn't seen it coming,
hadn't side-stepped and dictated the ground on which it
should approach him, and the terms on which he would
entertain it. Now it was too late to do anything but stop the
bleeding by force of will, and somehow claw his way back
to the job in hand. Because he had just established to his full
satisfaction that no man alive had a dog's chance of getting
within Maggie Tressider's guard. Want her as he might,
want would have to be his master, as it had been many
another's.

Or would it? If he played his cards intelligently, hadn't he
certain advantages?

She trusted him! She'd said so, and meant it. Who else
had her ear as he had? Who else had access to her as he
had? The hunt for X could be prolonged until his position
was secured, and the uncovering of X could be so handled
—assuming he was found, and in whatever circumstances—
as to serve the interests of Francis Killian no less than those
of Maggie Tressider. Yes, he had unique advantages . . .

And unique disadvantages, his own saner self warned him
tartly. You're taking her money to do a job for her, the only
trust she has in you is the trust intelligent people place in
competent professionals bound to them by contract. Take
one step out of line, to-morrow, next week, ever, and she'll
be gone. And you'll be a bigger heel even than you've ever
been before. At least until now you've kept your business
clean.

I shall still be doing that, he persisted strenuously, fighting off his better judgment. I'm not proposing to cheat her.
The job I've taken on for her I'll finish, if it can be done at

all. But while it lasts I've got her ear, I've got a measure of her confidence, and I'll earn more. I'm wronging nobody if I conduct my own campaign alongside hers.

And you think you've got so much as a dog's chance? asked his *doppelgänger* venomously. You know what that woman is, a world figure, a beauty, a towering artist. Do I need to tell you? And you know what you are, don't you? Or maybe you've forgotten. It's a long time since you looked in a glass!

There wasn't a mirror in the room, or in the flat apart from the one in the bathroom. But he didn't need a glass, he knew what he looked like, and what he was. A man of forty-one, average height, light weight, not bad to look at as average men go, if he hadn't spent all his adult life being knocked about by circumstances, and knocking himself about when circumstances let up. All that kept him from looking and being seedy was the odd vein of austerity that persisted from his Nonconformist upbringing, still unsubdued after a life-long battle with chaos and self-indulgence, and that basic dislike of dirt that would have been glad to believe itself a virtue, but sadly realised it was no more than a foible.

Yes, agreed his demon, reading his thoughts, you've had things cleaned up for the past five years, from artistic squalor into monastic order, and it cost you plenty to do it, and you know damned well the value you put on it. There was going to be no more of that! How much of your soul will you still own, if you let love break in here now? Don't you recognise a disaster when you see one? Take a look round this cell of yours. It's more than it looks, it represents the only safety you've got, because it's the only order, it's what's left of your morality, it's your identity. Open the door and let love into that, and it'll kick the whole structure apart before you can say: Maggie!

And he knew it was true. Only a fool could welcome in the invader of his painfully-won privacy, and run to meet the power that humiliated and outraged what he had made of himself at so much cost. And for such an impossible hope! He knew, none better, that he would never reach her. If he regrouped his defences now, while there was time . . .

But there was no time left. It was already too late.

All right, he said defiantly to his double, sit back and watch. A little patience, a little craft, a nice mixture of blackmail and gratitude, and you'll be surprised what I can do, when I want something enough. What will you bet me I don't get her in the end?

And if you do, said the demon, with the finality of ultimate, unquestionable truth, what you get won't be what you want. It will be only to possess and enjoy, you know that, don't you? And spoil! Never to unite with her.

All right, damn you! said Francis, setting his teeth, *then I'll settle for that!*

CHAPTER III

So FROM THEN ON he had two people's interests to serve, Maggie's and his own; and for the time being they were identical. If ever the two interests should diverge, God only knew what he would do, or which of them he would put first. There was no sense in trying to anticipate the event, and no comfort, either.

Back to the business in hand, then. If X was an injured lover, he belonged somewhere at the threshold of success. Ever since she was twenty years old she had lived in the sun, known exactly where she was going, and needed no claws. The more he thought about it, the more he was left with two formative years, the last two she had spent under Paul Fredericks.

What wouldn't he have given to be able to question the old man, or even his sister who had worked with him? Perhaps especially his sister, for an elderly woman sees more of what goes on inside ambitious girls of genius than does a doting old man whose protégées they are. But they were both dead long ago. Francis had, however, the lists of names of those who had accompanied Maggie on her three tours with Freddy's Circus. He began with the last, in the autumn of 1955. The last for an excellent reason, because after it she had been invited to sing Cherubini at Covent Garden, and Freddy had acknowledged that she was ready. That was also reason enough why Francis should consider it first.

And there in the list, if he couldn't have Esther Fredericks, was the woman who had taken her place on the trip. Bernarda Elliot. Now Bernarda Felse. If Freddy had turned to her in a crisis, she must have a good head on her shoulders, as well as a contralto voice in her throat. And hadn't Maggie said that she lived—or had then been living—somewhere here in the Midlands? Felse is not a very common name.

He looked in the regional telephone directory. Felse is not a common name at all, he found. There was just one of them in the whole of two border English counties and a large slice of mid-Wales. George Felse, of 19 Prior's Lane, Comerford. In the circumstances it wouldn't be much of a trick to find out whether his wife's name was Bernarda.

It was; though most people, he discovered, seemed to know her as Bunty. And her husband—well, well, who would have thought it?—turned out to be a detective-inspector in the Midshire C.I.D. A far cry from Freddy's Circus to a modest modernised cottage in the village of Comerford, only a few miles out of the county town, and just in sad process of becoming a town itself. Thirteen years is a long time; George Felse must have been a bobby on the beat when this girl—and Maggie had said she was good—decided he was what she wanted most.

So it can happen!

Don't build on it, Francis, he warned himself grimly, it couldn't happen to Maggie. A little interlude of a few months—even a year or so—you might get if you're lucky and clever, but not a lifetime, don't look for it.

He called the number in the book. The voice that answered was lighter than Maggie's, and more veiled. "Yes, I'm Bernarda Felse. But how did you know?"

A good question, but for some reason a daunting one. He might have to be on his guard with a woman like that, in case he gave away more than he got from her.

"My name's Francis Killian. I got your name from Maggie Tressider. You know she's in hospital in Comerbourne, after an accident? I do private research for anyone who needs it, in connection with books, indexing, that sort of thing. While she's laid up, Miss Tressider is compiling material for a possible monograph on Doctor Paul Fredericks. She's using me to do some of the donkey work for her. I believe you knew him well?"

"I studied under him," said the distant voice, with pride, with affection, with gaiety; entirely without regret. "He was one of the world's darlings. But irascible as the devil! No, come to think of it, the devil wouldn't be, would he? Somebody ought to put Freddy on record, that's a fact."

"It would be a great help if I could talk to you about him. May I come over and see you, some time?"

"Any afternoon that suits you," said Bunty Felse. "Today, if you like?"

*

The moment he set eyes on her he stopped wondering if she had any lingering doubts about her bargain. She was one of the few people he'd ever seen who looked as if they had never regretted anything in their lives. She was about his own age, a slender person of medium height, with a shining cap of glossy hair the colour of ripe conkers, and a few engaging silvery strands coiled in the red here and there. Her eyes, large and brightly hazel, looked straight into his over the coffee-cups and declared her curiosity quite openly, and the effect their candour had upon him was of a compliment.

"Will she really ever do anything about it? . . . this book on Freddy?"

"Ah, that's another question," admitted Francis. "Not for

me to ask. *You* could, if you went to visit her. I think she'd be pleased."

"That," said Bunty, reaching for an ashtray from the bookcase, "one doesn't do. I have just about as much claim on Miss Tressider as I have on half the big names in music to-day—I once studied for three years under a man they all knew and valued. So did dozens, maybe hundreds of others, most of them as obscure as I am. No, I contracted out, and you can't have it both ways, and personally I've never even wanted to. Well . . . hardly ever, and then only for a day or so. I never really knew the girl, in any case. I was married some years before she even came to Freddy. It was only the accident of Esther's illness that made us acquainted at all."

"But you remember her? As she was then?"

"You wouldn't," said Bunty with the slow smile that made the freckles dance across the bridge of her short, straight nose, "be likely to forget her. I assure you she was already glorious. I may have contracted out myself, but I haven't lost interest. I knew what we had with us on that trip abroad. Freddy told me, for that matter, but I'd already noticed for myself. In a way I think that particular tour was the turning point for her. She suddenly realised her full possibilities. As if everything in her had discovered its pole and fixed on it for good. She turned her back on everything except music."

The phrase arrested his mind and his pen together; he had a couple of pages of notes on Dr. Fredericks by then, since that was where his interest ostensibly lay. By this time he could surely afford to manifest some curiosity of his own about Maggie.

"She had her first big successes on that tour?" he asked.

"She did, that's true enough. But it was more than that, something that happened inside her own mind. I should guess she had plenty of faith in herself when we set out. After all, it was her third trip with Freddy. But somewhere along the line she seemed to wake up fully, and after that she set her sights on the top of the mountain and started walking. And she's never looked back."

She had, though, in the end; but Francis kept that to himself. When death put its hand on her and stopped the breath in her throat on the operating table, and then changed its mind and withdrew from her after all, somewhere a forgotten window had opened and Maggie had looked back.

He closed his notebook on his knee, and sat looking at Bunty Felse over it for a moment of silence. Then he said: "Tell me about that particular tour. Where did you go? Where were the concerts held? Did anything out of the ordinary happen? Tell me everything you can remember about it."

The hazel eyes, dappled with points of brilliant green in the sunlight, studied him thoughtfully. Now was the time for her to say: "I thought it was about Freddy you were collecting material!" but she didn't say it. Whatever she saw in him seemed to her logical enough reason for the change of emphasis. She didn't even find it necessary to comment.

"I've still got the whole itinerary and my working notes somewhere. It was the only time I had the job to do, so I had to get it right. I did all the secretarial work, you see, bookings, bills, the lot, as well as keeping an eye on the girls." She got up, and went to rummage in the drawers of the bureau. She hadn't kept these papers as treasured souvenirs, apparently, or if she had they had long outlived her reverence for them, and found their way somewhere to the most remote corner.

"Did you have much trouble?" asked Francis.

She laughed. "Very little with the girls. There were only three of them, and they were all completely serious about their careers. Freddy's students usually were, or they didn't last long. There was more trouble with Freddy himself, actually, that trip. He was always excitable before concerts, and we had one rather turbulent member among the boys who was just beginning to get in his hair." She found what she wanted, somewhat crumpled at the back of a loose-leaf book, and came back to the coffee-table smoothing it out in her hands; a dozen or so sheets of quarto paper stapled together, a handful of hotel bills and a sketch-map of their route across half of Europe and back to Calais. She dropped the little file before him, and sat down again. "Take it if it's any help to you." Her eyes met his levelly, and still she refrained from comment. She had her own ideas about the nature of his interest in Maggie Tressider, and who was to say she was wrong?

"I'd like to, if you're sure you don't mind? I'll return it . . ."

"Don't!" she said, and smiled. "It was a nice thing to do, just once, more interesting in a way than when I went with him as a soloist myself. But I've finished with it now. I did just one Circus when I was nineteen, and then opted for marriage, and that was it. My son was seven years old, going on eight, that summer when Esther went to hospital. To tell the truth, I felt more flattered being asked to stand in for her than if he'd asked me to go back to singing. And my mother took over the family for me while I was away. Everything went off nicely, and it's something to remember. But it's a long time ago now."

"You were saying," prompted Francis, his eyes on the map, "that Dr. Fredericks was having a certain amount of trouble during the trip. Did something happen to upset him?"

"Nothing very surprising. There'd been friction for some time in that quarter. We came home to England one member short, that's all. One of the orchestra walked out on us in Austria. Well, one of the orchestra . . . he was our occasional 'cello soloist, too, we had to rearrange some of the programmes after he defected."

"I take it this was the turbulent one who was getting in the doctor's hair? Do you remember his name?"

She leaned over to take the crumpled papers out of his hand and flick through them for the typed concert programmes she had compiled so long ago. "Yes, here we are . . . Robert Aylwin. That's right, they called him Robin. He was quite a brilliant player, if he'd ever worked at it, but it was becoming pretty clear that he never intended to. He'd been with Freddy for two years, but that trip he was putting all his deficiencies on show, and it was plain he wasn't going to last much longer. I doubt if he'd have lasted that long, if he hadn't been such a charmer. That was probably his trouble, he was used to smiling at things and having them fall into his hands, not having to work for them. Music was too much like hard labour. He was getting bored with the whole thing, and treating it with distressing levity. With Freddy that was naturally heresy. They'd had words two or three times, and we all knew it. Nobody was very surprised when the boy just took himself off, one night between dinner and bedtime, and never showed his face again. There were rumours that he'd been misusing his respectability as Freddy's protégé for a little smuggling, and Freddy's conscience was such—not to mention his natural sense of outrage—that he really might have turned the boy in. If true, of course! But one could believe it. Probably not much wrong with him except this incurable light-mindedness, but that was enough for Freddy."

"You mean he just packed and slipped away without saying a word to anyone? Not even to one of the other boys?"

"Well, supposing there was anything in the smuggling rumour, and he'd come to the conclusion he'd better disappear, then he wouldn't take anyone in the Circus into his confidence, would he? He probably wouldn't in any case, he was a very self-sufficient young man, he ran his own show."

"And you've no idea what happened to him afterwards?"

"Not the slightest. He was never going to hit the headlines as an instrumentalist, he couldn't be bothered. We just went on with our schedule without him. Freddy made no attempt to trace him, after all he was over twenty-one and his own master. He probably drifted back home when he felt like it, or signed up with some small orchestra over there. He was the kind to fall on his feet, and he spoke both German and French, he'd get along all right. We weren't worried about him."

But the strange, the unnerving thing was that suddenly

Francis was worried about him. For no reason, except that the boy had been near to Maggie, and had walked away into a long-past evening and left no trace behind him.

"Didn't his family want to know what you'd done with him?"

"He had no close family, as far as I know. He'd been knocking about on his own for two or three years already."

"What was this boy like? You haven't a photograph?"

She shook her head. "No photographs. I had loads of publicity pictures at the time, of course, but obviously I didn't file them. It's a long time ago. I remember him as a very attractive young man, and well aware of it. Girls liked him." She added after a moment's thought: "He laughed a lot."

"And where did this happen . . . this walking out?"

"We were staying in a little resort in the Vorarlberg, a place called Scheidenau. You'll find it all in the papers there. Freddy always used the Goldener Hirsch as a convenient base for all our concerts round there—Bregenz, Bludenz, Vaduz, St. Gallen, Lindau, all those places. It's very near to the German border, and quiet, and rather cheap."

"And he walked out between dinner and bedtime? Just like that? Did you notice anything different about him at dinner? Nothing to show what he had in mind?"

By this time, he realised, she ought to have been asking questions herself, and the very fact that she was not had drawn him into deeper water than he had intended venturing. He smiled at her, shaking away the betraying tension of his own concentration. "It seems such an odd time to cut his moorings."

"All he seemed to have in mind at dinner," said Bunty, disconcertingly remaining grave, "was ingratiating himself with Maggie. He'd been paying her special attention for several days, that I do remember. Not that there's anything remarkable in that. She was . . . she *is* a most beautiful person. All our boys were a little in love with her."

He kept his eyes steady and faintly amused on hers, his hands placid on the papers they held, with an effort of will that left him no energy for speech for a moment. And he wondered if she could have hit him so hard and so accurately without knowing exactly what she was doing. Not out of malice, perhaps, just by way of experiment; there are other ways of satisfying one's curiosity, besides asking direct questions.

"I'm sure they must have been," he said evenly, when he had his voice under control again. Let her wonder, too, by how much she had missed her target. "And what about Miss Tressider? Did she respond?"

"Maggie had other things on her mind by then. She knew what she wanted. She was nineteen," said Bunty, "she liked being liked, and she was a very nice, patient, quiet girl who would in any case have been kind to him. But she never took her eyes from her objective, for him or anyone."

Her voice was gentle, deliberate and detached. It was more than time to work his way back unobtrusively to Paul Fredericks for ten minutes or so, and then take himself off, before he gave her more than he was getting out of her. She was altogether too perceptive. He managed his retreat with finesse, but finesse was not enough. Never mind, she had made it clear that she sympathised, and also held it to be no personal business of hers; and he was never going to see her again closer than across a Comerbourne street.

"Of course," said Bunty Felse disconcertingly, seeing him out at the door, "after all this time she may have changed."

*

It did not occur to her that there was anything to disturb her in this interview, for fully an hour after it was over. Her visitor was presumably what he purported to be, and it was only his misfortune that an aching preoccupation of his own had side-tracked him from the master to the pupil. If there hadn't been something she had liked about him she might not even have noticed, much less felt obliged to warn him that she had. But after he was gone her mind began to nag at the curious implications of their conversation. Surely everything he had learned from her about autumn, 1955, Maggie already knew at least as well, and he must have known she would need no help in recalling details, supposing that she was serious about this book. No, that probe had been for his own satisfaction. And granted he had his own unhappy reason for wanting to talk about Maggie rather than her teacher, why just that incident, and why with so much controlled intensity? Why dwell so insistently on Robin Aylwin, who was of no significance whatever? Why want a photograph of him? The more she thought of it, the more it seemed to her that their conversation had gathered and fixed upon that enigmatic young man with quite unjustified interest.

She had not been asked to treat the interview as confidential. So she told George about it over tea, as she did about most things that stirred or puzzled her. George, who had had a fairly boring day, listened to her with pleasure and affection, but with only one ear, until a single harmless word unexpectedly caused all his senses to prick into life together. He came erect out of a faint blue cloud of cigarette smoke.

"*Scheidenau?*" he repeated sharply.

"Scheidenau," agreed Bunty, opening her eyes wide. "Why? Ring a bell, or something? I must have mentioned it *ad nauseam* at the time, but of course it's a long time ago. Anyway, it's only a tiny little resort, nothing special about it. What made you sit up and take notice suddenly?"

"Who did you say this fellow was? The one who came to see you?"

"Name of Francis Killian, a sort of private enquiry agent from Comerbourne. I told you, he's working for Maggie Tressider, collating all this stuff about Freddy, she's thinking of doing a book about him."

"Oh, Killian, yes, I know the name. Never met him, but as far as I know he's all right. But how did you get on to Scheidenau? I'd clean forgotten you'd ever been near the place."

"So had I, until I got the records out to show him. Was that just a jab from your subconscious, when you sat up and barked Scheidenau?"

"That's it," agreed George amiably, blinking at her

through dissolving smoke. "It reminds me of a recurrent nightmare—Dom eight years old and in temper tantrums, and you twenty-nine and as pretty as new paint, shaking a loose leg in the Vorarlberg. I had the horrors all the time you were away."

"There wasn't a soul around you need have worried about," Bunty assured him scornfully, "even if I hadn't been up to the neck in bills and transport arrangements. Just Freddy, and all those callow young men years younger than me. Not to mention the competition! Only three girls, but two of them were presentable, and the third was a beauty. Still is," she said, abruptly recalled to the serious consideration of her afternoon's entertainment. "He's in love with her."

"Killian? With Maggie Tressider? How do you know?"

"Killian. With Maggie Tressider. And I know, all right. Oh, he wasn't obvious in any way, but there it was. I liked him," said Bunty, who always knew her own mind, and added, relevantly enough: "Poor boy!" That he was her own age, within a year one way or the other, did not invalidate the sentiment. "I knew you weren't listening," she said, "I told you all this."

"I'm listening now. Tell me again."

She told him, well aware that this was not a game. She had touched some recollection which had nothing at all to do with her own stay in that remote Austrian village.

"And he never showed up again, this Aylwin chap?" said George, when she had reached the end of the story.

"You know, I never once thought of it in those terms. He wasn't any greenhorn, he spoke three languages, he knew his way around. I would bet he made his own erratic way wherever he was going, and is playing that 'cello of his somewhere around Europe now. But no, I suppose he didn't show up again anywhere *we* went, at any rate. Why? What makes him suddenly so interesting to everybody?"

"Just that he disappeared in Scheidenau. That would be how long ago? Twelve years? . . . thirteen. Because it so happens," said George, handing over his cup for a refill, "that another young man failed to come home from a continental holiday just a couple of years ago. A Comerbourne young man, which made him our case. An art student named Peter Bromwich. Stepfather works at the power station, mother has a job at the ordnance depot out at Newfield. Twenty-three years old, off on his own with a rucksack. He knew the answers, too, it wasn't his first trip by several, and he was a bit of a know-all by inclination. But he didn't come home, and nobody's heard of him since."

"In Scheidenau?" asked Bunty, now very grave indeed.

"Not quite, not this time. Bromwich was last seen on the German side of that border, trying to thumb a lift towards Immenstadt. From then on he just vanished. We made pretty wide enquiries at the time, and more police forces than you can imagine got into the act, since so many borders meet around those parts. German, Swiss, Austrian, even Italian. Nobody found Peter Bromwich. What we did find, when we all got our heads together, was that an awful lot of major and minor mysteries had dwindled away into dead ends just where all those frontiers tangle, over the past ten years or so. Some were currency cases, some were drugs, some were stolen valuables, mainly small but first-class stuff, jewellery, antiques, art pieces. Two escaped convicts from an Austrian gaol disappeared off the face of the earth in 1960 after being chased as far as Langen—not the Arlberg one, a little place up there near the border. A suspect wanted for murder in Munich was traced to Opfenbach, and then completely lost. Quite a remarkable collection of loose ends, as if they'd originally tied up neatly into a skein at the eastern end of Lake Constance, and somebody had sheared the knot clean out and got rid of it. And not a thing there to think much about until we got the lot together, because a case or two in one country's records, that's not so impressive, but a dozen together begin to look like something above lifesize. But nothing ever led anywhere, and Bromwich never reappeared."

"And the case is still officially open?"

"Very much so. And I'd still be more than interested in

closing it. It did emerge that Bromwich was on Cannabis, and may have graduated to the hard drugs, and there were indications that he might have brought the stuff through Customs with him at least a couple of times before when coming back from holidays. It looked rather as if he'd got himself tangled into the fringes of some sizeable organisation. Maybe this time he got a little too cocky? Or too curious about his employers? Now I suppose there wouldn't be any such indications in the case of your young Aylwin, would there?"

"In a small way," admitted Bunty, "there would. Not drugs, though, I'm sure. If Freddy'd had any such suspicion he'd have turned him over to the police like a shot, and my impression is that he just intended to get rid of him and leave it at that. There were *rumours* that Freddy had accused him of taking advantage of his position as one of the Circus—so respectable as we were, you see!—to get away with some petty smuggling. I took it to be simply the little personal luxury things everybody's tempted to try and sneak in once in a while. His real crime—or disability, rather —was that he simply couldn't take life, or music, or even Freddy seriously."

She sat back to consider, with a dubious frown, the picture she had just painted, and it did seem to her, on reflection, that there might be a basic similarity between these two troublesome young men.

"You think *he* may have stumbled into waters too deep for him, too? Chanced his arm with somebody dangerous, and come off worst?"

"Or blundered into something dangerous by accident, and failed to get clear? There are, of course, other possibilities. Maybe he's still hitch-hiking his way round the world somewhere at this moment."

"That," said Bunty, though without conviction, "is the ending I prefer."

"It's the ending Peter Bromwich would have preferred, I don't doubt. But I very much doubt if it's the end he came to."

They sat silent for a moment, eye to eye. They could see deeper into each other than most people, and it was often like looking into a glass, their minds moved with such unanimity.

"But why," asked Bunty then, "was it the name Scheidenau that brought all this back to you now? Peter Bromwich was some miles away in Germany when he was last seen."

"He was. A good point! I told you we turned up, between us, any amount of other queer cases that ended in blanks, all roughly round that eastern end of Lake Constance. It occurred to Duckett once, when he had nothing better to do, to link them all up into a squashy sort of circle and see what he got. And then, just for the hell of it, he plotted the centre. And whether it means anything or not, where do you think it fell?"

"Scheidenau," said Bunty.

"Scheidenau. A tiny little dot on the map that nobody'd ever heard of, but that's what he got. Maybe if we plotted the exact centre of the figure described by linking up all last year's bank raids, it would drop on Windsor Castle. But still my thumbs prick. Scheidenau once may well be a freak, and I might even have had a lurking suspicion that my dear chief didn't do his sums right. I never checked! But Scheidenau twice, and do you wonder I have the feeling that fate is nudging me?"

"But this man Killian *is* working for Maggie Tressider," Bunty said positively. "That's true enough. He suggested I should go and visit her, he isn't afraid of his credentials being investigated."

"Oh, I don't doubt that. But he may be working for her on something rather different from what he gave you to understand. He seems to have spent more time asking you about the lady herself than about her teacher."

"Yes, I know. Though we'd already been talking about Freddy for some time. But it's natural he should want to talk about Maggie. I told you, he's in love with her. Even this fixation about Robin Aylwin . . . I had a feeling even that was a personal thing with him. As if jealousy was eating him alive, and he had to find somebody to bear the burden, somebody round whom he could crystallise it and get rid of it. And when I talked about Robin, good-looking and close to her, and her own age, for the first time—and I'm sure it *was* the first time he'd so much as heard of him —he felt he'd found a possibility. Somebody to resent. Not that it helps," said Bunty wryly, "but they always think it will."

"God forbid, love," said George piously, "that you should ever feel the urge to psychoanalyse me. I hate to think what you might come up with. No, I'm not suggesting there's anything wrong with Killian or with Miss Tressider, I should say it's very long odds against it. But if her commission, whatever it may be, is turning his attention to the disappearance of a young man in Scheidenau, then I'm very, very interested. It might be well worth while keeping an eye on his moves. Even if he doesn't find what he's looking for, he may accidentally turn up something interesting to us. I'll try to get a look at him myself as soon as I can. What's he like?"

She told him. It appeared that she had been weighing up Francis Killian's physical attributes as acutely as his state of mind, and the odds were that she was pretty accurate about both.

"Fortyish, middle height, on the thin side but I think he's solider than he looks. Dark brown hair and eyes, thick brows, hair a bit grey just at the temples. Quite a good face, clean-shaven, a lot of bone and not much meat, a long, straight nose and a rather high forehead. Daunting way of looking at you, guarded and aloof but critical, too, as if he held you at arms'-length to get a stranger's view, and didn't want to get any closer to anyone. Slumps his shoulders a bit, but when he's on his feet he moves well, so it may be an affectation. Or pure discouragement! He did look rather as if he'd nearly given up, and then suddenly got kicked back into the race. Not quite seedy—he's physically too trim for that—not so much a shabby elegance as an elegant shabbiness."

She had closed her eyes, the better to see the man who was not there. When she opened them they were bright, thoughtful and clear. "How's that?"

"Strictly for the fiction shelves," said George rudely, and tucked away mentally every word of it. "Now supposing— just supposing—you wanted to get to Scheidenau quickly, and money was no object. How would you go? Air to Munich . . . Zurich . . .?"

"Zurich," said Bunty promptly. "Could do it either way, but Zurich would be quicker and easier." She sat looking at him wide-eyed, a shining mirror reflecting his thoughts back to him. "I happen," she said cautiously, "to be on rather good terms with Laura Howard in the B.E.A. office in Comerbourne. I could have a word with her. Very discreetly, of course. What did you mean about money being no object? He didn't look as if it would be no object to him."

"If she's retained him to do a job for her," said George, "Miss Tressider will be paying the expenses. And *if* he takes off for Austria after your long-lost 'cellist, the quick, expensive way, that should clinch one thing, at least: he'll be following up this line on *her* business, not his own."

"But we," said Bunty, now with unmistakable regret, "shan't be able to follow him there."

"Too true we shan't. But we just might, with a lot of luck, get an inkling of what, if anything, he brings back with him."

*

The violinist who had shared Robert Aylwin's room at the Goldener Hirsch in Scheidenau, thirteen years ago, lived now in Birmingham, and played in the City of Birmingham Orchestra. Bunty's working papers of the tour had proved very useful indeed, supplying the names Maggie had forgotten, and even such day-to-day details as room accommodation. Charles Pincher and Robert Aylwin had been roommates throughout, so they must, if not friends, have been reasonably congenial companions. Why should Maggie remember the one, apparently the less memorable, and forget the other?

Mrs. Felse had said clearly and kindly that Maggie had not been interested in Aylwin or in any man, and probably never would be. But Mrs. Felse might be mistaken. And still Francis saw, or thought he saw, the shadowy outline of a person round whom his bitterness could gather corrosively, a man who must have meant something to her, probably much, perhaps everything, if she hadn't disastrously mistaken her own heart, and kicked away love too hastily from trammelling her feet on the climb to the heights. Why else should she fasten so suddenly and hungrily on fame, why come back changed, unless she had not merely turned her back on the alternative, but herself destroyed it?

So he went to see Charles Pincher. And Charles Pincher, tall, stooped, balding and cheerful, remembered the Scheidenau affair very well.

"There was one rather odd thing about it, you know. He didn't take anything with him when he lit out."

Slowly Francis closed his notebook on his knee. "He didn't . . .? You mean he just walked out empty-handed? But Mrs. Felse said nothing about that . . ."

"No, well, I don't suppose she ever realised. But his suitcase and his 'cello were there in the room still, after he'd gone. Freddy left them in old Waldmeister's charge when we left, he said he'd be sure to come back and collect them as soon as he knew we'd gone, and the bill was paid."

"*And did he?*"

"I suppose so, old boy, but I was never there again. I had the chance of a good job, so I quit the Circus. I expect he did, you know. We all knew he'd fallen out with Freddy. He'd just keep out of sight until we were on the move, and then stroll back and pick up his traps at leisure."

The sensible thing to believe, of course. The only question left was whether it had actually happened like that.

Whether, in fact, there had been some sound reason why it couldn't happen like that. And there was only one infallible way to find out, and find out quickly.

*

"We were right," said Bunty over the telephone to George."Zurich! Laura booked him in on the two o'clock Trident flight from Heathrow to-morrow. Open return. Took him a day and a half to make up his mind."

"Now I wonder," said George at the other end of the line, "I do wonder to whom he talked yesterday, and what they told him, to make his journey really necessary?"

CHAPTER IV

THE LITTLE SCHEIDENAUERSEE, a silver-blue pear-shape three-quarters of a mile long, lay in green folded hills under a late summer sky, smooth as a looking-glass and brushed clean with feather dusters of cloud. Its narrow end, where the tiny Rulenbach flowed into it, pointed south into the foothills of the Vorarlberg, and round this southern tip the village of Scheidenau lay, three short streets arranged in a Y shap, the cup of the Y filled with the water of the lake as with silver-blue wine. The northern end of the lake widened and overflowed from the cup, mirroring two or three tiny islands, and at the north-eastern corner the Rulenbach flowed gaily out again, twice its former size and bouncing down a crumpled, stony bed, to make an unexpected six-mile detour through Germany, owing to the complicated contours of the land, before returning into Austria in a series of right-handed twists, to empty itself into the Bregenzer Ach, and eventually into Lake Constance south of Bregenz.

Where the three streets met there was the usual village square, with a well-head and a modest Trinity column in the middle, and on all three sides—for in fact the square was an irregular triangle, dwindling towards the south into the stem of the Y—the beautiful, exuberant housefronts and shopfronts, the overhanging eaves, the mellow dark wood and virtuoso wrought iron that makes almost any small Austrian settlement look like a stage set for operetta. There was a baroque church, of no particular merit but of pleasing appearance, one restaurant that was not also an inn and two that were, and a confectioner's noted for its rum babas. All the down-to-earth shops like the butcher's and the baker's and the ironmonger's, lined the landward street. The two roads that embraced the end of the lake, and dwindled later into footpaths along its undulating shores, found room for the villas and gardens of the better-off, for a small public park nestling in the base of the Y like the dregs of the wine, and for the two larger of Scheidenau's three hotels, which peered into each other's windows across the placid surface, just where the arrow-straight clay-blue line of the Rulenbach's inflow, coloured by mountain water, foundered and became invisible in the deeper, calmer blue. The third and smallest hotel, the Weisses Kreuz, faced the church across the broader end of the square.

Outside the village the farms and fields began, rolling, heaving, foothill fields white with the shaven stubble from which the harvest had been taken, and upland pastures scalloped like fish-scales from the marks of the scythe. The highest point visible from the square was the abrupt hummock of the castle hill just to the west of the lake, with its snaggle-toothed ruin on top, meanly reduced now to its last few feet of broken wall and a tangle of overgrown rubble, useless as a tourist attraction. Outcrops of bedrock and outcrops of masonry spattered the sides of the hill over an area of a square mile or so, and because of the rich rooting of trees and bushes it was sometimes difficult to tell which was which. In parts of the forlorn shell the practical natives had dumped rubbish, and there were rats as the only inhabitants; but still that scattered rash of worked stone erupting everywhere among the grass bore witness to the formidable extent of the place in its hey-day. The Waldmeisters, who owned the Goldener Hirsch, and had been there now for seven generations, took their name from an ancestor who had once been head forester to the Lords of Scheidenau.

The Goldener Hirsch, sprawled along the lake-shore on the western arm of the Y, with its shoulder turned solidly to the remnant of old splendours on the castle mound, was in a curious state of suspension between village *gasthaus* and tourist hotel. To the huge traditional house, with its beetling eaves, strongly battered walls, built-on cattle-byres and carved wood verandahs, had been added a new wing in brick and stone, in an austere modern style that did not offend. Two Waldmeister daughters, still unmarried, and the wives of the three Waldmeister sons, continued to run the place with a couple of poor relations and almost no outside staff; but there was a smart little reception desk in the hall, with a smart little Austrian blonde in a mini-skirt seated behind it, darting like a humming-bird between her typewriter and adding machine on one side, and the telephone switchboard on the other.

It was already September, and the high season dwindles away very rapidly when August ends. Yes, she had a room and a smile for the unexpected Englishman who had made no reservation. But the woman who showed Francis up to his room wore the full, flowered skirt, embroidered apron and laced bodice of old custom, and had her mane of black hair coiled on her head in the old heavy bun, and to judge by the waft of warm milk and cattle-flesh that drifted from her skirt as she walked ahead of him up the scrubbed wooden stairs, she had just come in from the cows.

The first-floor corridor was wide enough for a carriage and pair, the door she flung open for him broad enough to admit them two abreast. All-white, high ceiling, spacious walls, huge billow of medium-weight autumn feather-bed on the creamy-white natural wood bedstead. He was in the old part of the house; so much the better. The window looked sidelong on a large, ebullient, untidy garden, and only a sliver of the lake winked in at him. No room in the world could have been more at peace.

"The gentleman is English?" His German had been hesitant, and in any case the unmistakable stamp is always there, for some reason. He owned to his Englishness; he might as well.

"The room will do?" Her voice was low, abrupt and vibrant, curiously personal in uttering impersonal things.

"The room will do beautifully, thank you." He dropped his bag on the luggage-stand, and felt for the keys of the hired car in his pocket, and the loose change under them.

"A moment! I will open the window." The scent of her as she passed near to him was like the wild air from outside, part beast, part garden, part earth, part late summer foliage ripening towards its decline. She turned her head suddenly as she passed, so close that her sleeve brushed his, and he saw her face full, olive-dark and olive-smooth, and the great, bold, sullen, inviting eyes for once wide-open and glowing. But the next moment she was looking round the room with the glow veiled, and the faint, dutiful frown back on her brow.

"No towels. I will bring."

She was, he realized, a very striking woman, her tall figure as lithe as an Amazon, her features good, her hair splendid. Until he had looked at her so closely he had failed to notice that there was a flaw, for her articulation was so clear that there seemed to be no malformation in her palate. Only that small, vicious botch put in to spoil the pattern and embitter her life; her upper lip was split like a hare's. The effect was not even ugly, prejudice aside; but prejudice is never very far aside from the hare-lip in an otherwise handsome woman.

She came with the towels, and he took them from her at the door. Her fingers touched his in the act. He was sure then that it had not been by accident that her breast, braced high by the black bodice, had brushed his sleeve as he had stepped past her into the room on entering.

"If you should need anything, please call for Friedl. I shall be working below. I shall hear."

"Thank you, Fräulein Friedl. I'll remember."

Her eyelids rolled back for an instant, and again uncovered, so briefly that he could believe in it or not, as he
chose, the buried volcano. Probably she had not much hope,
but as a gesture of defiance against the world she persevered
and deployed what little she had.

"You are Herr Waldmeister's daughter?"

The hare-lip quivered in what was not quite a smile. "His
niece," she said, and walked away along the great, scrubbed
corridor with her long stride, and left him there. But the
slow, swaying walk, the erect back, the beautifully balanced
head with its sheaf of black hair, all were still quiveringly
aware of him until the moment when she passed from
sight.

So that was one of the amenities, and one that wouldn't
be in the brochure, nor, he thought, available to everyone.
Some special kind of chemistry had elected him. One cast-
away hailing another, perhaps, for company in a huge and
trackless sea. One insomniac welcoming another in the long,
lonely, sleepless night.

He washed, and went down into the bar. There were
voices in the garden and boats on the lake. Across the
shining water the windows of the Alte Post blinked languidly in the sun. There were still plenty of visitors to
keep the natives looking like deliberate bits of folklore—
which emphatically they were not—but in a couple of
months the stone-weighted roofs, the beetling eaves, the
logs stacked beneath the overhang ends-outwards, all up
the courtyard walls, would no longer look like window-
dressing, but a very practical part of the seriousness of
living. Soon the stocky, old-gold cattle with their smoky
faces would come clanging down from the high pastures to
their home fields for the winter.

The scrubbed boards of the floors were almost white in
the guest-rooms. It was early afternoon, the quietest hour of
the day in the bar, but there were a couple of obvious
French guests sipping coffee and *kümmel* in one corner, and
a bearded mountain man with a litre pot before him was

conducting a conversation with the woman behind the bar, clear across the width of the room in the booming bass-baritone of the uplands. The woman was middle-aged, grey-haired and solid as a wall, and could be no one but Frau Waldmeister.

Francis ordered an *enzian*, and went straight to the point. She heard him broach his business, smiling at him a benevolent, gold-toothed smile, but as soon as legal matters were mentioned she did exactly what he had expected her to do, and referred him to her man. That saved him from having to go through the whole mixture of fact and fiction twice, and got him installed in a quiet corner of the empty dining-room, across a table from the master of the house. Old Waldmeister was something over six feet tall, with shoulders on him like a cattle-yoke, and a wind-roughened leather face decorated with a long, drooping, brigand's moustache. Courteous and impassive, he listened with no sign of surprise or suspicion at being suddenly asked to think back thirteen years.

"Herr Waldmeister, my name is Killian. I am representing a firm of solicitors in England, who are looking for a certain young man. A relative of his family resident in New Zealand has left the residue of his small property to him. The dead man had been out of touch with his cousins in England for some years, and we find now that the legatee parted company with his parents some time ago, and they have no idea where he is at the moment. We have advertised for him without result, at least so far. We therefore began to make enquiries in the hope of tracing him. The last record we have of him, strangely enough, terminates here, in your hotel, thirteen years ago."

He waited to elicit some sort of acknowledgment, and what he got was illuminating. The first thing old Waldmeister had to say was not: "What was his name?" but: "How much is it, this legacy?"

"When cleared, it should be in the region of fifteen hundred pounds." Not so great as to turn out the guard in a full-scale hunt for him, but great enough to pay the expenses of a solicitor's clerk as far as Scheidenau, in these days of off-peak tourist bargain travel. The old man nodded weightily. Property is property, and the law is there to serve it.

"How is he called, this young man?"

"His name is Robert Aylwin."

"I do not remember such a name. *The last record* of him, you say? It is a long time ago. To remember one visitor is impossible."

"You will remember this one, when I recall the circumstances." And he recalled them, very succinctly and clearly. There were names enough to bolster everything he had to say. Fredericks had regularly used this inn on those tours of his; neither he nor his students would be so easily forgotten. "I understand from a man called Charles Pincher, who shared a room here with him, that Aylwin left his suitcase and his 'cello in the room when he went away, and that Dr. Fredericks gave them into your charge, expecting the owner to come back to collect them. Is that so?"

"It is so," said the old man without hesitation. "The name I had forgotten, but this of the cases and the Herr Doktor, that I remember."

"In that case I'm hoping that you can help me to the next link in the chain, that he gave you at any rate a forwarding address, when he came back for them."

"He did not come back for them," said Waldmeister, and volunteered nothing more.

"He didn't? Then in all these years you've had no word from him?" The chill at the back of his neck, like icy fingers closing there, made Francis aware that he had never believed in this. Considered it, yes; believed in it, no.

"No word. That is right."

"Did you . . . expect to?" What he meant was, did you know of any reason why it would be no use expecting it.

"I expected, yes. People do not just go away and leave their belongings. You understand, it is a very long time since I have thought of this matter. No, he did not come, and I knew no way to find him. I kept the things for him, that was all I could do. But he did not fetch them."

"Then . . . you still have them?"

"Come with me!" said the old man, and rose and led him from the room, out to the broad stone passage-way with its homespun rugs and its home-carved antique chairs and spinning-wheels and boot-jacks, over which a London dealer would have foamed at the mouth. Up the uncarpeted, scrubbed, monumental back stairs, spiralling aloft with treads wide enough at the wall end for a horseman to negotiate. One flight, a second, a third, and they were up among the vast dark rafters, in a series of open attics that hoarded rubbish and treasure together in the roof.

"Here," said Waldmeister simply, and pointed.

The 'cello-case, leaning sadly against a scratched wooden box, might have been covered in grey felt, but when Francis drew a dubious finger along its surface the blanket of dust came away clean from a finely-grained black leather. Of good quality, expensive, and surely almost new when the owner abandoned it here. A medium-sized black suitcase, its upright surfaces still almost black because it was of glossy, plastic-finished fibre-glass, stood beside the 'cello.

"This is his? May I look? Under your supervision, of course. All I want is to see if there is anything there to suggest a further line of enquiry. Are they locked?"

"They are not locked."

Of course, they would be as he had left them in his room, and in a hotel room which is itself normally locked, not everyone bothers to make doubly sure with individual keys. And the keys themselves he must have taken away with him, in his pocket.

The contents of Robin Aylwin's luggage had little enough to say about him. He travelled light. The slacks, lambswool sweater, shirts, were good but not expensive, and kept about as carefully as most young men of twenty or so keep their clothes. Black dress shoes for concerts, a dinner jacket, shaving tackle, handkerchiefs, a Paisley dressing-gown, pyjamas, a Terylene raincoat, all folded and packed so carefully that Francis detected the hand of some female member of the Waldmeister family.

"Had he packed these? Or were they simply lying about in his room?"

"They were in his room, as in use. We packed everything as you see it, to wait for him."

No passport, no documents, no wallet, no keys, no letters. All those he would most probably keep on him, whatever clothes he was wearing. The dinner jacket being here meant nothing; he almost certainly wouldn't wear it for the evening here, when resting between engagements. Probably it was only there for the concerts. There were writing materials, a folder of stamps both English and Austrian, two local postcards, unwritten; but not one written word, to him or from him, to help to establish that he had ever really existed at all.

Francis got what he could from the remnants. The shirts were size fifteen and a half, the shoes nine, the slacks were long-legged and small-waisted and made to measure, but from a firm of mass tailors with shops everywhere. The wearer must have been nearly six feet in height, if not an inch or two over, and on the slim side, though by the evidence of the sweater, which was a forty-two inch chest, he had needed accommodation for good wide shoulders. And that was all there was to be discovered about him here. The 'cello, silent in its case, was just a 'cello, and the pockets that filled in its curves contained only resin, strings and a spare bridge in case of damage.

Francis closed the lid again and restored the case to its corner. He dusted his hands and looked at Waldmeister.

"No, nothing. When he didn't turn up, I expect you looked through them, too."

"I also told it to the Herr Doktor, when he came again. He knew nothing of the young man, either. He said keep them still, so we kept them."

"Herr Waldmeister, there is always the possibility that

some member of your household may have talked with
Aylwin while he was here, and may be in possession of some
detail that might help me to find him. It's a long time ago,
and your staff may have changed, of course, but still there
may be someone who remembers, and may be able to add to
what we know. Will you be kind enough to tell them, all
those who were here at that time, that I am trying to trace
this man, and for a reason which makes it to his advantage
that I should find him?"

The old man's heavy shoulders lifted eloquently. "I will
do so. But I do not think, after all this time, they will have
anything to tell."

"I'm afraid you may be right. But please ask them to
come to me if they do remember anything. I shall be here
for two or three days."

"I will ask them," said Waldmeister.

*

He had reckoned on the force of curiosity to bring them
to him even if they had nothing to tell, and would have bet
on the women being in the lead. But the eldest Waldmeister
son was the first to bring his stein over and join the new-
comer in the bar, after dinner that evening. He could surely
have nothing to tell about a chance guest in the hotel, since
he spent all his time well outside it, running a timber business which was merely one of the multifarious Waldmeister
activities. What he wanted was to have a closer look at the
English solicitor, and at least offer his desire to be helpful,
if he could do no better. Frau Waldmeister and two of her
daughters-in-law made roundabout approaches during the
next day, to the same effect. None of them knew where
Aylwin might have gone, none of them knew why. Francis
doubted if they really remembered anything about him at
all, beyond that he had left in the attic tangible evidence of
his stay. The third daughter-in-law hadn't then been married to her Johann, and the two youngest Waldmeister girls
must have been still at school.

The one person for whom he had trailed the bait held
aloof. Friedl, somewhere in her mid-thirties now by his esti-

mate, must have been turned twenty at the time, and not the
girl to miss a personable young man. Aylwin had been, by
Mrs. Felse's testimony, of striking and engaging appearance, and even at twenty Friedl, the dowryless niece with the
hare-lip, must have been half-way to the hungry, embittered
woman she was now. Deprived enough to reach out for
whatever man she could, and not yet crushed into acceptance
of her lot, and schooled to limiting her reach to waifs like
herself. If anyone here knew anything about the good-looking and light-minded young man who laughed a lot, the odds
were it would be Friedl.

He knew she would come. She was only biding her time.
He had caught her dark, sullen glance upon him several
times in passing, but she had made no sign. He understood.
Where the Waldmeister family was within earshot or sight,
no one would get anything out of Friedl. They were perhaps
hardly more the enemy to her than was the rest of the
world, but she would make no move where they might get
wind of it. It was not a matter of the importance of anything
she might have to say, but rather of preserving the integrity
of her own secret life, which had nothing to do with them.
She might have nothing to tell, but she would come, all the
same, given the chance, because he had, and deliberately,
offered her a reason for approaching him.

There was no real difficulty. After dinner was cleared
away he sat with a *kirsch* on the verandah that overlooked
the tip of the lake, until she came out, off duty at last, to
enjoy the luminous air of the evening. He had seen her
emerge the previous night at this hour, and he felt reasonably sure that it would be the same to-night. All she had
done was to stroll in the garden and talk a little with such
guests as were solitary, but she had done it in a smart black
wool dress, with a gold chain and cross round her neck, and
her great mane of hair coiled in a glossy chignon on her
nape; a manifestation at least that she did exist as a human
being, like them.

She was a little later in appearing to-night, but she came.

As soon as he saw her in the doorway, Francis moved away to the rail of the terrace, where the steps led down into the long slope of trees between the inn and the lake-shore. It was already dusk, but the afterglow had turned the western sky to a pale, glowing green, and its reflection from the lake, calm as a looking-glass laid down among the hills, cast a subtle radiance up through the trees. Without haste and without looking back, Francis went down the path.

The Goldener Hirsch stood on a bluff, higher than the Alte Post on the other side of the lake, but equally close to the thin yellow line of gravel that bordered the water. Sixty yards wide and gradually broadening as he penetrated deeper into it, the belt of trees wound along beneath the balconies and windows of the new wing, and the path, narrowing, wandered diagonally down it to the water. Not there, it would be too light there. Somewhere here in this curious woodland world quivering and swimming in greenish gleams, like a weedy aquarium. He had already left the evening strollers behind. There might be a pair of lovers holed up somewhere in the twilight, but there was room for them. He let the path slip right-handed away from him, towards the dappled, moon-pale water, and took to the grass beyond, moving at leisure among the trees. He didn't know how far behind she might be, but he knew she would find him.

He lit a cigarette to simplify the process for her, and the act shook him for a moment into full consciousness of what he was doing. He was on Maggie's business, and if there was anything here to be found he must find it. He needed Friedl's testimony for Maggie's sake and for his own. But Friedl had her own needs, and as good a right to make use of him as he had to make use of her. Whichever way you look at it, he told himself derisively, you're not going to find anything to be proud of, and since when have you started breaking your heart over a bit of necessary, ambiguous disloyalty? Get what you have to get, and pay whatever you have to pay for it. That's what Friedl will be doing. Maggie will never know. *You* will, of course, but what sort of drop will this be in the ocean of what you know already about yourself?

He felt her close to him before ever he heard or saw her. His senses homed on the awareness he had that she was there, and then he found the tall, motionless darkness, the two pale flowers of hands quiet at her sides.

"Herr Killian . . ." A muted breath hardly as loud as a whisper; and not a question, she knew who was there.

"Fräulein Friedl . . ." he said as softly.

She crossed the few yards that still separated them, and as she came the greenish, reflected light flickered over her face twice, tremulous and faint; it was like seeing a drowned face float through clear, shallow water. Thus delicately touched, Friedl achieved beauty. The flaw did not show at all, the enchanted light brushed her weatherbeaten skin with its own liquid jade.

"Herr Killian," said the dream-like murmur, "I can tell you about the man called Aylwin . . . if you want to know . . ."

"Yes . . . yes, Friedl, I want to know . . ."

He went the necessary, the imperative step to meet her. She walked into his arms.

*

"The last time I sat here with a man," she said, drawing fiercely on the cigarette Francis had just lit for her, "it was with him. With Robert Aylwin."

They were sitting on a felled tree in a half-circle of bushes some distance along the lake-side, looking out through a filigree of branches over the water. She had brought him there by the hand, moving like a hunting cat, silent and certain in the dark.

"They were here three, four days. He was nice to me. We came to this place together. He was not like me, he was gay, always gay."

No one, thought Francis, could accuse us of that particular indiscretion. Something was there with them, heavy and fatal, something of warmth and tenderness and bitterness and pity that left an indescribable, rank flavour on the night. But most surely no gaiety.

"Aylwin had been here two or three times with Dr. Fredericks," he said. "Hadn't you met him before?"

"I was not here until that summer. I came when my father died. I had nothing, you understand? Not even a human face. Who would want me? But he was lively, and funny, and kind. On that last evening I was late finishing the dishes, and I saw him go out, across the terrace, down the path . . . as you did to-night. And when I was finished I followed him."

"You had an arrangement?" asked Francis, lifting the heavy sheaves of her unbound hair in his hands.

"No, we had no arrangement. Simply, I hoped he might come here and wait. But before I reached this place, a little way back there among the trees, I heard his voice. And another voice. A girl's . . . So I drew back a little, not to break in on them, but it was quiet there, and I was among the bushes. I didn't want them to know, and I could not get away quickly because of the branches . . . they would have heard me . . ."

His throat was dry. "Could you see them?"

"No. It was also September, and a little later in the evening. No . . . but both voices I knew. His, of course. And hers . . . you could not mistake it, even speaking. She was the one from his own party, the one they said was going to be a great singer."

He heard his own voice saying with careful concentration, for fear he should frighten her away from the issue by too great an intensity: "Could you hear what they were saying?"

"No, most of the time not. All was in undertones, and it was he who talked, and she who listened, only now and again she said some few words, and with her it was impatience and disbelief . . . you know? He was arguing and pleading. And she did not want him, she was sending him away, but he would not go. At the end he forgot to be quiet, he cried out loudly at her: '. . . if *you* don't want me!' And she said, 'Hush, don't be a fool!' And he said: 'No, I won't be fool enough to endure it. *There's always an alternative!*' That is what he said, and like that. Do you think I could imagine that?"

"No," he said. His voice felt and sounded thick and muffled in his throat. "No, I don't think you could." Carefully, carefully now, or she would catch the spark of passion and take fire, and he would get nothing more. "And what did *she* say?"

He never knew what it was that betrayed him. Not the voice, that was level and light, interested but detached, under complete control now. Not even the mere fact that he should ask after *her* reactions, when it was in Robin Aylwin's movements he was supposed to be interested. Something deeper and more fundamental than any such details, something she felt through the almost indistinguishably altered tension of the arm that circled her, a dark lightning striking from his blood into hers. This was a creature who felt with her blood and thought with her bones and flesh, and saw with some intuitive third eye under her heart like a child. For suddenly all the air was still about them, with something more than mere silence, and very slightly and stealthily all her sinews drew together, contracting into her closed being, lifting the confiding shade of her weight from his shoulder. She did not move away from him; she did not even lift her head. It would have been less frightening if she had. But all the essence of herself that she had spilled so prodigally about her on the night air, as securely as if she had been alone, drew back like ectoplasm and coiled itself defensively within her. There was a third person there, almost palpable between them.

"She laughed," said Friedl in a clear hard voice.

"No . . .!" he said involuntarily. There seemed to be two Friedls there now, one of them warm against his shoulder with the black waterfall of her hair streaming across his chest, one of them standing off at the edge of the clearing, watching him narrowly, waiting to see him react in anger or pain. There was not much she did not know now, in that dark blood-knowledge of hers, about his relationship with the absent woman who had laughed.

"*Yes!* You wished to know about him, I am telling you what happened. Nobody else can tell you, nobody else knows. She laughed at him, that girl. And then I heard the bushes crashing as he turned and ran away from her, down towards the lake. Only for a few moments, because the ground drops there, and this hillock where we are cuts off sound. There was this thrashing among the bushes, and sometimes his feet stumbling against a tree-root, and then it was quiet because he was down there close to the water, under the curve of the ground. But if there are voices in a boat on the lake, then you hear them. That night there were no boats, no voices, it was already dark. It was another kind of sound we heard, that girl and I, coming up from the water. A splash. Not so great a sound, clean, not broken, not repeated . . . but all the same, it was not a fish rising, even though there are very big fish in the lake. It was too late, too dark, and besides, one gets to know all such sounds. No, this was something, something heavy, plunging into the water and going down . . ."

She had turned in his arm, tensed and brittle against him, and he felt her eyes searching his face even in the dark, experimental, inimical and savage. Suddenly the night had engendered, seemingly out of her very flesh, a small, murderous wind that chilled him to the bone.

"I don't believe you," he said, "you're making it up."

"You think I am lying? Ask *her!* When you go back to her, ask her!"

"You're crazy! What have I got to do with a woman like that? If this had been true you'd have told somebody about it then. Did you? Did you go down to the water to look for him? Did you tell what you knew when he failed to come back?"

"What did I know? What did I *know?* That there were voices, that I heard a splash, nothing more. No, I never told anyone I was here in the trees that night. No, I did not wait to see, I did not try to find out anything. I ran back to the

house, and I held my tongue. *And so did she!* Why should
I speak? I wanted no part in it. What did I owe to any of
them? Better to be quiet and keep out of trouble. So they
never dragged the lake, they never even looked for him, he
was simply the one who was out of favour and ran away.
But *something* went into the lake that night. And she heard,
as I did, and wanted not to hear, as I did, but with better
reason. And he never came back for his baggage, did he?
And he never will!"

She drew herself out of his arm suddenly and roughly.
"I've told you everything I know. I must go back."

"I still think you're lying," he said, but without anger,
and without conviction, only with an almost insupportable
weariness and sadness.

"Then ask her, when you go back to her. You will see."

He could have denied Maggie a second time, but what was
the use? Friedl was as sensitive as a dog to the presence of
ghosts.

"Help me do up my hair. They will be looking for me."

He stood behind her and drew back the great fall of her
hair, smoothing the sheaf between his hands; and then for a
moment her hands were on his, guiding them, her body
leaned back against him warm and yielding, and she turned
her head and laid her cheek against his. Without movement
and without sound she was weeping.

"Friedl . . ."

"No . . ." she said. "You cannot help . . ." Silenced under
his kiss, her marred mouth uttered one lamentable moan,
and clung for an instant before she pulled herself away. She
thrust the comb into her heavy coil of hair. "Don't come
with me!" she spat back at him, and was gone, abrupt and
silent between the trees.

CHAPTER V

So NOW HE KNEW what lay at the bottom of Maggie's memory like truth at the bottom of a well. She, too, dazed and enchanted with her vision of fame, impatient with the importunate boy who blundered into her dream in defence of his own, had heard that muted splash round the curve of the lake-shore. And she had chosen to bury it, not to understand, not to remember. Not because she didn't know what she had done, but because she did!

Surely she must have loved him!

All the way across Switzerland in his hired car, Francis was eaten alive by the knowledge. What else could explain the obsession that rode her now? Nothing less than love, recognised too late, could have made this disaster so terrible to her. And yet there was some excuse for her. There had never been any proof, never any body, everyone else had taken it for granted that Aylwin had simply decamped, and their acceptance had made it the most reasonable course for her to accept that probability, too.

Only in her heart she knew that he hadn't!

Every time the knowledge surfaced she must have thrust it under again, until at last it drowned, and stayed down. Her conscious mind had succeeded in sloughing the memory utterly; but deep below the surface something in her had relentlessly remembered and reproached and grieved, and at the point of death had bestirred itself again to struggle into the light and challenge her with her debt.

He lingered a day in Zurich because he didn't know what he was going to do, what he wanted to do, what he could bear to do. And about Friedl he thought only once during that time, with a violent tearing at his own conscience, and the shock of realising that the suppression of what galls and accuses is not so difficult or rare. That we all do it. That life would be impossible if we did not.

On the second day he asked for a passage home, but had to wait one more night before getting one. He was glad of the respite. Because what *was* he going to do about Maggie? No use trying to shield her by lying to her, she was utterly sincere when she said she wanted the truth, that she couldn't live without truth. Did he even want to spare her? There were times during the flight when he realised that he wanted rather to rend her, to make her pay not only for Robin Aylwin, but for his own self-torment, too, and even for poor Friedl, with the tiny blemish on her flesh and the great cancer in her spirit, and the men who had slipped through her fingers because Maggie was innocent and dedicated.

He telephoned the hospital in Comerbourne as soon as he landed. He still had no idea what he wanted to say. It was almost a relief to get the ward sister, brisk and cheerful and immune, explaining that Miss Tressider had made rapid progress and was now discharged. Yes, she was still in Comerbourne, she could be contacted at the Lion Hotel, where she had taken a suite for a period of convalescence under supervision. She had wanted to have a grand piano, an amenity the hospital naturally couldn't provide.

That was no great surprise. The voice that used her as a means of communication was restless and fretful, aching for an outlet again. Had she, after all, had any choice when she kicked love away from her? Wasn't she, from the moment she realised the incubus that rode her, a woman possessed?

He telephoned the Lion Hotel.

"Yes . . . Oh, *yes*!" she said. The voice, full, clear and eager, drew her upon the air in front of his eyes. "Yes, much better, thank you! Do come! I wondered about you. I shall be looking forward . . ."

*

"I've been following," he said, with the even delivery of a machine, "the course of that last tour you made with Dr. Fredericks." He dared look at her only briefly and occasionally, because the blue of her eyes blinded him, so vivid and wondering and hopeful they were upon his face. "I stayed at a small resort called Scheidenau, near the German border. Do you remember it?"

"Yes, vaguely. There was a lake . . . and a castle . . ."

"And a small hotel called the Goldener Hirsch."

"You mean the one Freddy used to take us to? I'd forgotten the name, but I remember how it looked."

The Lion Hotel was by the Comer bridge, and her suite was above the waterside. The tremulous light, reflected from a high ceiling and white walls, shimmered over her face, which was clear and pure as crystal, without shadows. She looked marvellously more substantial than when he had seen her in her hospital bed, but still fine-drawn and great of eye, and the tension that held her seemed more of hope than fear, as if the very act of sending him out to probe her disease had somehow absolved her and set her well on the way to a cure. Perhaps for a few days, in his absence, she had even begun to feel that setting out to look for the answer was the same thing as finding it, that now she could take up her life again, that the crisis was over.

He approached her not with clear statements, but with promptings, for what seemed to him a good reason. For Friedl, in spite of her reckless challenge to him to go back to his Maggie and ask her outright, might still have been lying. And supposing he confronted Maggie with this story, and still her memory failed or refused to fill in the blank spaces, so that she could never positively know whether the thing had happened like that or not? The last thing he wanted was to burden her with a grief she had not deserved. So he came towards his point by inches, waiting for a spark of understanding and enlightenment to kindle in the blue, attentive eyes; and the name he held back to the end. If she spoke it first, then they would both be sure.

"That was a very important tour for you, wasn't it? You had your first great successes, and you knew what they were worth. You began to see a really great future ahead of you, quite rightly. Do you recall anything else of importance that happened to you on that trip?"

"In Scheidenau?" She was watching him closely, her lips parted. The faint hint of an eager smile quivered and died, two pale flames of anxiety burned up in her eyes. He saw her fine brows draw together, painfully frowning. "I can't think . . ."

"In Scheidenau. On the last evening before you left. No? In the woods along the shore of the lake, below the hotel. There is a maid at the hotel named Friedl, a niece of the family. You remember her?"

She was harrowing all the recesses of her mind for anything that could account for his gravity. Every line of her, from the long fingers tightly clasped in her lap to the pearly curve of the skin over her cheekbone, strained thinner and whiter with mounting tension. "Please!" she said. "If you know something, tell me!"

"Are you sure," he said harshly, "that you want to know?" He had meant to be gentle, but the rage and pain came up into his throat like gall. And now not only was she afraid, but also there was something deep within her stirring in response to his passion, tearing her in its frenzied attempts to get out, the deep-buried knowledge heaving into wakefulness at last. It was on its way to the light, and nothing could keep it imprisoned now.

"Yes, I want to know."

"Friedl says that she was in that strip of woodland that night, the night before the Circus was due to leave. She says that she heard two people talking there, and that one of them was you. The other was one of the boys who toured with you. She says that he was arguing and pleading his cause with you, and that you were trying to get rid of him. She says he cried out at you that *something* would happen 'if you didn't want him!' He said—she remembers the words—: 'I won't be fool enough to endure it. *There's always an alternative!*' . . ."

Maggie's lips moved, but there was no cry. She clutched the edges of the stool and leaned forward, trying to rise. He would never forget the sudden blind, blank stare of her eyes, lancing clean through him after another face, another accuser.

". . . and then he ran away from you down the slope towards the lake, and she heard—and *you* heard, didn't you?—the splash of something falling into the water. And he never came back, that night or ever . . ."

She was torn suddenly erect before him, the convulsion of knowledge passed shudderingly through every nerve of her body and flamed into her eyes. She clutched her cheeks hard between her palms, and a wailing cry came out of her, thin and lamentable:

"Robin!"

He would not have believed that she could ever utter such a sound, or he provoke such a sound from her. Sick and mute, he stood and stared at his work. Whether she wanted the truth or not, they both had it now, and there was no shovelling it back into its grave.

"Robin!" she said in a rustling whisper. "So he never came . . . But how could I have known? He wasn't any responsibility of mine . . . was he? *Was he?*"

She had appealed to Francis, and therefore she became aware of him again, no longer as an apocalyptic voice ripping away the layers of her forgetfulness one by one, but as a man, a live human creature shut in there with her, and one who knew more about her than any man should know. All that long-buried burden of her guilt lay there in full view between them. They looked at each other across the wreckage with horror, anger and hatred. Each of them knew what the other was seeing, and each recoiled in outrage from the violation of privacy involved. Nothing was hidden any longer, everything assaulted Maggie's lacerated senses at once, his love, his resentment of love, his humiliation and rage at the invasion of his bleak solitude. Both his love and his antagonism were unbearable, and there was nowhere to hide.

Her body, newly schooled in the use of weakness where there remains no other weapon, found the only way of escape. Francis saw her deliberately, resolutely withdraw from him into the dark, and sprang across the room towards her a second too late. She let her hands fall, and dropped like a crumpled bird.

*

She came round in his arms, on his heart, aware of his agony before ever she heard his voice panting and whispering her name. Fingers light and agitated and gentle smoothed back the tumbled hair from her eyes. A broken and contrite murmur entreated her:

"Maggie, forgive me . . . forgive me! Oh, my God, what have I done?"

She lay like a dead woman, and made no sign. It was the only way to keep any part of her integrity free of his touch, of his love which she did not want, of his nearness which affronted her, of his pain, of which she was mortally afraid. No one must come this close to her, no one touch her with this wounding fervour. She must get rid of him. He must know no more of her, he already knew too much. So she kept her eyes fast closed and her spirit tightly withdrawn from him, even when the shadow of his face stooped between her and the light, and he kissed her on the mouth. The touch shook her to the heart with pity and panic and distress. She held her breath and remained apart.

"Maggie, speak to me . . . look at me . . ."

Suddenly he was up from his knees and plunging away from her across the room. She heard the faint single ring as he lifted the telephone.

"No!" She opened her eyes and raised herself unsteadily among the cushions of the couch, where he had carried her. "No, please don't! I'm all right . . ."

He spun on his heel, and for an instant she saw such abject hope, relief and solicitude in his eyes that her head swam again. Then she felt as a convulsion in her own flesh the effort with which he drew down over his face the austere mask of professional detachment he normally showed to the world, and hid his nakedness from her. She thought wretchedly, we've destroyed each other. This proud man will never forgive me for frightening him so far off-course into humility and self-betrayal, any more than I can forgive him for penetrating so far into my jungle, and caring too much about what he found. What affair am I of his, outside the terms of the agreement? And what right had I to find my way under his skin and reduce him to this?

"I was going to call your doctor. I think I should."

"No, please hang up. I don't need anyone. I don't want anyone." She sat up, smoothing her dove-grey skirt. "I'm sorry I alarmed you," she said. "It was only a momentary weakness. I shall be all right now."

"I'm afraid I've upset you too much. I wish you'd let me call someone."

"Please, no, it's quite unnecessary. Now, if you'll be kind enough to hand me my bag . . . It's there on the piano . . ."

He brought it, handing it to her with fastidious carefulness, not to touch, not to make any claim upon her, now that she was awake and aware. Her pallor was less extreme now, her face was calm, almost cold. The fear was gone and the hope was gone; she was past the moment of impact, it seemed, and beyond there was an emptiness, an area of shock, where as yet nothing hurt and nothing comforted.

"Don't worry about me, I shall be quite all right now. I'll lie down and have a rest, after you leave. Thank you for all the work you've put in on my case, you've been most efficient, and I'm very grateful." She was riffling through the contents of her handbag, her head bent; and in a moment she looked up at him, holding out a sheaf of notes. "I hope I've reckoned up right. This is only the fee for the actual number of days, of course, including to-day. Please let me have the amount of your expenses, they must have been considerable. Don't trouble to itemise, I shall be quite satisfied with a round figure. And again, thank you!" Very courteous, very low, very final, that wild-silk voice of hers, dismissing him; but so gentle that at first he hardly understood, and when he did, he could not believe.

"You mean you're dispensing with my services?" His face was whiter than hers.

"But surely, you've completed your assignment very successfully. I asked you to find out for me what it was I'd done . . . to feel that I had a death on my hands. And you've done it. There's nothing else I need."

"You're accepting this without examination? I should have thought we needed to go into it in detail, to satisfy you that it's authentic. I was too brutal, I beg your pardon! I wanted to avoid mentioning names, to see if there was any genuine memory of this incident . . ."

"You have seen," she said, "that there is. It needed only to be uncovered. There is no mistake. And I am quite satisfied."

He stood gazing down at her, and felt time and the world grinding to a stop, and only a blank before him. She continued to sit there, pale, resolutely withdrawn into herself, holding out the sheaf of notes patiently in a hand that trembled a little from weakness; and her eyes had become the heavy, opaque blue of Willow Pattern china. There was nothing he could do. He was not going to plead with her for a small corner somewhere in her life, and he could not force his way where she did not want him to go. He had not even the right to turn on his heel and walk out, and leave her holding the money she felt she owed him. He was a hired employee, commissioned, paid off and dismissed. What could he do but take his fee, and go?

"I ought to point out," he said, in a voice almost as dry as the desert he saw ahead of him without her, "that what I've reported and what you may have remembered is not enough to prove what actually became of this man Aylwin. You yourself know that there were completely logical reasons for believing, as Dr. Fredericks certainly did, that he had simply walked out. Granted that you have additional knowledge, you still have no proof that Dr. Fredericks' version is not the correct one. For all the real evidence anyone possesses, Aylwin may be very much alive and perfectly well. If you won't allow me to follow up the possibilities for you, at least remember that."

Did he for one moment believe what he had said? Certainly she did not. Perhaps now she knew more than he did. She remained marble-still, the notes extended gravely in her hand.

"Thank you, you're very kind. Please believe that I appreciate what you've done for me, but there's no need to follow it up any farther. And now, I'm a little tired . . ."

He could not keep her waiting any longer. He took the money without a glance, and thrust it into his pocket.

"May I know . . . what you intend to do?"

"I have no plans," she said.

"If there should be anything further to tell you, can I rely on finding you here?"

"For a while, yes. I don't know how long."

"If you should need me, you know where to reach me." She did not offer him her hand, and he did not expect it. He walked to the door without looking back. "Good-bye, Miss Tressider!"

"Good-bye, Mr. Killian!"

The trouble was that he didn't mean it, and she did. Wherever she looked for help, out of friendship or for hire, never in this world would she turn to Francis Killian again. She had crossed him out of her experience, buried him as deep as the body he'd dug up for her. After the compromising intimacy of what they'd just done to each other, he thought grimly as he walked down the stairs, it was either that or marriage.

*

He had taken her money, because he had had no right to refuse it, but now that he had it, it was his business what he did with it. He walked into the church opposite the hotel, and cast a sullen eye over all the almsboxes, but the combating of dry-rot and death-watch beetle and the financing of overseas missions in countries arguably more moral and likeable if not more Christian than England did not appeal to him as a job for Maggie's money. He went down to the Salvation Army shelter by the embankment, where they had

a permanent collecting-box on the wall outside, in the form
of a giant tambourine, with his favourite appeal written
across it in large, cheerful characters: HELP UP THE DOWN-
BUT-NOT-OUTS. He pulled out the untidy wad of notes from
his pocket, and stuffed them anyhow through the slot.

A disinterested-looking man sauntering past with his eyes
apparently on the river took in this surprising act, and
loitered to lean on the rail and the embankment and think it
over, as Francis stalked away.

George Felse had been following him ever since he had
shouldered his way through the revolving doors of the Lion
Hotel and butted savagely through the traffic into the
church opposite. It was a chance meeting only, in fact
George was on his way to the car-park where he had left his
car. But the apparition of Bunty's visitor, back from
Austria and striding stony-faced and hot-eyed away from
an encounter with his principal, had lured him out of his
course. Everybody knew from the local evening paper that
Maggie Tressider had taken a suite at the Lion; and by this
time George had studied Francis Killian's photograph too
thoughtfully to miss that face when he saw it cross the
pavement in front of him. First the almsboxes in the church,
and now this startling treatment of a fistful of money. And
the desolation and rage in the worn, illusionless face. It takes
a lot to wound a man without illusions. It takes a touch of
madness to make most people throw money away.

George walked to his car slowly and thoughtfully. Whatever Maggie Tressider's commission had been, it looked as
if it was over. And there at the Salvation Army shelter her
agent had jettisoned his pay, in anger and offence. Was it
possible that Bunty had been right about him? Had he a
far larger stake at risk?

And might it not be well worth while, so far as other
duties allowed, continuing this unofficial watch upon him?
In fact, upon both of them?

*

It was on Saturday, the fourteenth of September, that
Laura Howard telephoned from the B.E.A. office.

"Bunty? Something rather intriguing—if you're still interested in your party? He looked in yesterday afternoon, and asked me to do exactly what *you* asked me to do! He wants to know if *Maggie Tressider* books a passage anywhere. He knows I shouldn't do it but he was in dead earnest. And of course, I didn't promise, not exactly, but remembering what you said last time . . . Well, I didn't say I wouldn't, either. I thought I'd better consult you, and see what was on. Because, you see, *she has*! This morning! She rang up and wanted a passage to Zurich next Wednesday, and I've got one for her on the 16.10 from Heathrow."

Bunty had waved George over long before this point, and his head was inclined intently beside her own, listening to the distant clacking with ears stretched.

"Well, I mean, *Maggie Tressider*! But he seems on the level, and he says he's been working for her. Has he?"

"Yes," said Bunty, "that's right, he has."

"Then what do I do? Should I let him know?"

"Ask her," hissed George, "if there's another flight to Zurich the same day."

"Hallo . . . Laura? Is there another flight that same day?"

"Lots . . . 10.10, 10.50, 14.10 . . . and tourist night flights, of course . . ."

"Tell him," breathed George, "and a thousand to one he'll be on one of 'em if there's a vacancy."

"Yes, Laura, tell him. He's O.K. And Laura . . . let me know if he books a crossing for himself, will you?"

"Oh, well," said Laura philosophically, "in for a penny, in for a pound. O.K., I'll call him. And I'll call *you*, double-quick, if there's any trouble." She rang off.

Bunty cradled the 'phone, and gazed round-eyed at George over it. "*Now* what's going on? It doesn't make sense for him to be peering round corners and suborning B.E.A. employees to find out what his own client's up to. He can't have been lying about working for her, because he wasn't at all worried about the possibility that I might pop out and buy some flowers and go round to the Royal to visit her. In fact he suggested it. And plenty of people would have, especially after being told she'd remembered them. Now it seems he's expecting her to go running out there herself, and not to say anything to him about it. So what *is* going on?"

"I rather think," said George, "that they've parted brass-rags." He recounted the incident of the Salvation Army shelter. "It looks as if he brought *something* back with him, and something that got him paid off and sent about his business. And somehow I don't think it was book material about Paul Fredericks, do you? Anyhow, he wasn't a bit happy about the result, you should have seen his face! And he certainly got rid of her money so fast it might have been scalding him. But now it does seem that he hasn't exactly accepted his dismissal, doesn't it? Far from it, he's still going to be bloodhounding along after her wherever she goes, unless I miss my guess. Only this time unknown to her, and unpaid."

"I told you," said Bunty, "he's in love with her. If she's going to walk head-on into trouble, he's going to be on the spot to pull her out of it."

"And you think she *is* going to be walking into trouble?" demanded George, of himself at least as much as of his wife.

"It looks as if *he* thinks so. And after all, he's the only one who knows what he found there, isn't he?"

"You're so right," agreed George ruefully. "I only wish he wasn't. I'd give a good deal to be in the know myself." He sat mute for a few moments, his eyes fixed on Bunty in bright speculation; she knew him so well that she could almost see him making up his mind. "Bunty, how would you like a few days in the Vorarlberg?"

"Us?" she said, startled. "You and me? You mean follow them over and keep an eye on them?"

"*If* he decides to go after her. Yes, you and me—why not? I've still got a week of leave to take, some time, why not now and why not in Scheidenau? If nothing comes of it, we've lost nothing and had a holiday. And if something does come of it, if he's turned up something about the dis-appearance of your young Aylwin . . . Well, who knows? If we roll one more stone over we may find Peter Bromwich, too. I'd give a good deal to close that case."

"We couldn't travel on the same flight with either of them," pointed out Bunty. "*He*'d know me, for certain. And *she* just might."

"I was thinking rather of hopping over with one of the tourist night flights, ahead of them. They won't all be fully booked, not in September. And it would give us time to lay on a car from Zurich, ready to trail those two as soon as they land. Train or road, we can tag along once we've got them in our sights. What do you say?"

Bunty reviewed her responsibilities, and could find nothing against it. Dominic and his Tossa wouldn't be home from their student trek in Yugoslavia for a fortnight yet, just in time to head back to Oxford.

"I say yes, let's!" said Bunty with enthusiasm. "*If* he follows her, of course," she conceded with a sigh.

It was late afternoon when the telephone rang again.

"Bunty? Laura here! How did you know? He's booked on the 14.10, two hours ahead of her!"

CHAPTER VI

SECOND COUSIN GISELA, of the mini-skirt, the blonde ponytail and the white wool knee-stockings, heard the car drive through into the courtyard of the Goldener Hirsch, and whirled her stool round to see who was arriving. The French couple from the second floor had left this morning, and most of the currency-starved English were already gone. The slight chill of approaching autumn fingered thoughtfully at the roofs of Scheidenau. A new arrival was not only profit, but entertainment, too.

The driver, a frequent visitor here during the season, brought in two cases of modest size but excellent quality, and his manner indicated that he had been more than adequately tipped. Gisela reviewed the accommodation she had to offer, and looked up with hopeful brightness as the new arrival came into the hall. English, a lady alone, very beautiful, very pale, very fragile. She wore a fashionably simple little tube of a dress in fine wool jersey, printed in rich warm tones of rust and amber and peach that did their best to reflect some colour into her face, but Gisela could see that without that reflected glow she would have been ashen, with lavender hollows in her cheeks and deeper violet shadows under her eyes. Her clothes, from the narrow black shoes to the small, gold-rimmed halo of a black hat, spoke of money. Her face, white, remote and abstracted, seemed not to belong to the picture, even though everything she wore had been carefully chosen to set it off at its best. Gisela had the feeling that she had seen that face before in magazines, and that it was famous and ought to be recognized, but the firmament of opera and the concert platform was not her world, and she had no memory for the stars that revolved in it.

The voice which asked for a room was very quiet and a little husky with fatigue, yet it was the most vital, vigorous and live thing about the visitor, as if it used and drove everything else. A voice that would make you prick up your ears and turn round to see if the face matched it, even if you heard it simply ordering beer in the bar.

"How long will the lady be staying?"

"I don't know . . . several days. If I'm not asking for impossibilities, I should like to have a piano to myself somewhere. I have to practise," she explained with the shadow of a smile, "and I don't want to disturb anyone."

Gisela was eager. "If you would like it, there is a suite on the first floor which has a large sitting-room. To-morrow they could bring up a piano for you from the dining-room, there are two there. Only an upright, but it is a good tone, and in tune." The suite was the dearest apartment in the house, and someone who wanted a piano as part of the amenities could well afford to pay for it.

"Upstairs?" said Maggie doubtfully. "I shouldn't like to

put them to so much trouble. Won't it be very heavy and difficult?"

"The stairs are so wide and so shallow, there is no difficulty. Like a castle, you will see. And the suite is very nice, it looks over the lake, and has a verandah with steps down to the grounds. I will show you." And she whisked open the flap of her desk, picked up the two suitcases like handfuls of feathers, and started sturdily up the length of the vaulted hall.

Maggie followed the straight young back and twinkling white wool legs to the vast rear stairs, and along a broad, echoing corridor on the first floor. She had no conscious memory of anything here, yet she knew where something was changed. It was like revisiting the place of a dream, or perhaps even more like dreaming of a place so uncannily familiar as to convince her she had dreamed it before. On those long-past visits with Freddy she had slept far up on the third floor, in rooms appropriately cheap for aspiring young performers. This large blue and white room, with its verandah blazing with geraniums, the airy bedroom opening from it, the bright hand-made cover on the old, carved bed, these she had never seen before. She went out into the open air and leaned over the flowering rail, and the scent of the trees came up to her, and the glimmer of the lake refracting light to her invisible, in small, broken darts of paler green launched through the deep green dusk.

"Dinner is over," said Gisela, "but if you would like something to eat I will tell them. You are very tired, shall we not bring you something here?"

Maggie sat down on the edge of the bed, and its firm softness drew her like a magnet. "I am tired. Yes, if you would be so kind, it would be very nice to eat here."

"And you like the room? It will do?"

"It will do very well. But I haven't signed, or filled in a card for you."

"To-morrow," said Gisela cheerfully. "And in the morning they will bring up your piano. Everything to-morrow!"

And she went darting along the corridor, in small, light thumps like a terrier running on the naked boards, and skittered down the stairs back to her switchboard.

Maggie undressed, her movements clumsy with exhaustion, wrapped herself in a housecoat, and lay down on the bed. The feather coverlet billowed round her, cool and grateful, closing her in from the world. There were no thoughts left in her at all, only this terrible weariness suddenly eased and cradled, and sleep leaning heavily on her eyelids the moment she lay down.

Only this morning she had left Comerbourne for London, picked up fresh clothes at her flat, and taken a taxi out to Heathrow in time for her flight. Then the train journey on to Bregenz, and the car to bring her up here to the border. And ever since Zurich, places and scenes familiar to her throughout the years of her fame had taken on a different, a remote familiarity, as though the nineteen-year-old Maggie had come back to savour them with another palate. A bitter taste, perhaps of poison. I am not yet well, she told herself, I see, hear, feel with distorted senses. But in her heart she knew that it was because all these places were populated now by one more person, many years forgotten.

It was five days now since she had remembered Robin living, and been brought face to face with Robin dead. Five days in which he had kept her company every step of the way.

She was discharged to her own care, she could go where she chose and take the responsibility for herself. None the less, she had gone gently and gradually about this pilgrimage, concentrating her forces to satisfy her doctors that she was fit to travel, and assuring them that her intention was to take a leisurely, convalescent holiday at a resort she already knew well, where she would be comfortable and well-cared-for, a complete rest that would set her up to tackle life again. Turning her head on the pillow and catching sight of her own drawn face in the glass, she felt certain she had not looked like this when they agreed to let her go.

She must remember to send Mr. Rice a card full of reassurances to-morrow. Everything to-morrow!

She had done certain other things during those five days: cancelled a few more forward engagements, answered all her letters, arranged a transfer of money to the accounts of Alec and Dione, in case they found themselves in difficulties while she was absent.

"While she was absent" was how she phrased it in her own mind; but before she left England she had also made her will.

*

Across the water, in a room on the second floor of the Alte Post, Bunty Felse lowered the field-glasses from her eyes with a crow of satisfaction, and turned to meet George as he came into the doorway behind her.

"She's here, all right," he reported. "Came up in a car from Bergenz not a quarter of an hour ago, and turned up towards the Goldener Hirsch."

"I know," said Bunty, "I've just seen her. Those are her windows, almost opposite to us, see? With the flowers and the balcony. The curtains are drawn now, but when the girl brought her up and put the lights on they were open. It was the lights that made me look there. I might have mistaken the face at this distance, even with glasses, but I couldn't mistake that hat."

She had never been quite easy in her mind since they had taken their eyes off that hat, a thin gold halo in the back window of the taxi, on the road from Zurich airport, and allowed Maggie to be carried away towards the town without them. George had had to make a snap decision which of the two to follow, for the middle-aged hired Dodge with Francis Killian at the wheel had swung unhesitatingly north-east on the fast road to Winterthur.

"He knew where she was heading, all right," said George, focusing the glasses on the pattern of lights over the water. "And which hotel she'd make for when she got here. Lucky we followed him in by road, or we wouldn't have known which one he'd picked for himself. As it is, you'll be able to keep out of his sight here without any trouble."

"I wonder why he did choose the Weisses Kreuz, when this one is so well-placed for keeping an eye on her?"

"He couldn't know she'd have that room, could he? And the Weisses Kreuz is on the corner where all the roads meet, all traffic going up to the Goldener Hirsch has to pass it. He was there on the terrace," said George, "waiting for her to arrive. When the car went by, he paid and strolled off in the same direction."

"You think he'll try to see her?"

"No, I think he'll want to see without being seen himself. He won't want her to know he's spying on her, not if you're right about his feelings for her."

"So we wait for him to move," said Bunty, "and *he* waits for *her*. And *she*, I shouldn't be surprised, waits for somebody else, I wonder who?"

*

Maggie, on her way down to breakfast, met a woman on the broad white spiral of the back stairs, a tall woman in traditional dress, with black hair plaited into two great, shining braids and coiled high on her head. She was carrying two heavy cases as she climbed, so that her head was bent, and that tower of glistening hair was the first thing about her to catch Maggie's attention. She drew aside to where the steps were narrowest, to let the burdened woman by, and because she was still a little shaky and hesitant from the fatigue of the previous day, she halted and held by the wall rather than risk proceeding on the tapering treads. The woman's eyes travelled upwards steadily from the narrow, elegant black shoes to the smooth russet-amber hair. Her head came up like the head of a deer scenting man. For a moment she halted, motionless and silent, and the sidelong light from a window accentuated the cleft in her lip, scoring the shadow there cruelly deep.

Maggie and Friedl stood mute and intent, gazing at each other. Thirteen years is a long time, but a hare-lip on an otherwise good-looking girl is bitterly memorable, and to be world-famous is to have one's photograph penetrate everywhere, if any reminder was needed. And even more surely, there stood between them the shadow of an absent third, at once a link between them and an impassable barrier.

"You are the lady from Number One?" said Friedl, with a gaunt smile in which her eyes played no part. "Franz and Joachim will bring up the piano for you this morning."

"Thank you!" Maggie hesitated for a moment only. "You are Fräulein Friedl?"

"How kind of the gracious lady," said Friedl, "to remember me." The smile, returning, hollowed her brown cheeks and raised a hungry gleam in her eye that was neither gracious nor kind. "It is a long time ago."

"I must speak to you," said Maggie.

"Not here. Not now." Friedl watched the colour ebb and flow on the too-prominent cheekbones, and slow, burning resentment gathered about her heart and ached insatiably. This was the woman who had and did not value the devotion of every man who set eyes on her, while she, Friedl, beautiful of body but marred of face, provided a passing interest for such men as had nothing better to do, but was never noticed, never regarded, as a woman in her own right. Wait, she thought, there is always a price on everything, and you've had so much and paid so little yet! "I have my work to do," she said. "I am not a daughter of the house."

The tone was mild and even servile, but the eyes were inimical, and even the note of self-abasement had its implicit reverse of smouldering arrogance. Maggie shrank. If she could have turned back now she would have done it, but there was no way of turning back. It was even possible that this woman knew no more than she had told Francis; but if she did, Maggie had to know it. There might be no comfort in knowing, but not to know was to be balked of her own identity. She had come here, tidying up her affairs behind her, and leaving no dependent of hers unprovided, simply in the determination to know; there was no other thought or ambition left in her mind.

"When may I have a talk with you?" she asked patiently.

"I am not free until after dinner. And even then, if we wish to be undisturbed, better it should not be in the house."

"I will come wherever you choose."

"This evening, when I am free, I will go along the path to the wood, under your verandah. Come out by that way, please, after me. They do not like it if I mix too much with the guests." It was a lie, but so well did it fit into the picture she was composing of an oppressed poor relation that she almost felt it to be true. I will make you follow me, she thought, as I followed him. I will take you where I took him, and make use of you as he made use of me. And I'll hurt you as he hurt me, and with interest. When I'm done with you, you shall have one man round your neck for life, and go the rest of your way ringing him like a leper's bell to keep every other man off, for fear of bringing him to the same end. I know your kind!

"Very well," said Maggie. "I shall be watching for you. I'll come."

*

"What more do you want?" said Friedl harshly. "*He* told you all this, didn't he? That man you sent here. Here in this very place he asked me what you have asked me, and I told him. And what did you need with either of us to tell you? Who knew better than you what sent Robin rushing down the slope there and into the lake? Yes, you had the right to refuse him, if you didn't want him, yes, you could tell him to go away—am I blaming you? What was it to you if somebody else loved him, and wanted what you didn't want? But you cannot have it both ways. If you think you did him no wrong, why do you come weeping back like a penitent, asking to be forgiven for killing him? If you did nothing shameful to him, why are you ashamed?"

In the half-circle of bushes, with the night deepening round them, all colours on the landward side had become an opaque wash of olive green. Against the faintly luminous shimmer of lake and sky, thinly veiled by a lace of branches, Friedl in her black dress prowled restlessly. The slight rustle of her feet in the grass frayed at the silence when her voice ceased. Somewhere a twig cracked. She reared her head to listen, frozen in mid-stride. The moment she was still the ultimate silence flooded in and possessed the world.

"No . . . Nothing! No, nobody else ever comes here at night."

She came a step nearer, turning her back on the lake, and stood black and tense against the pallor of the sky.

"I loved him. You understand? For two days, just two days, I was his mistress. But he never thought seriously of me. What man ever did? *You* were there, you with everything. How could he even see me for long? You don't believe me?"

"I believe you," said Maggie. "I am sorry!"

The sense she had had on the staircase of something rank and bitter and unprovoked assaulting her had become here an emanation of horror, unrelieved by the breeze or the cool of the air. For the first time in her life she knew it for hate, and was helpless in face of it. The tall darkness seemed to grow taller, hanging over her malignant and assured. It was not fear that held her paralysed, but a sick revulsion from the proximity of such hatred, an intuition that if it touched her she would never feel clean again.

"It is late to be sorry. Why did you not call him back then? Why did you never tell what you knew?"

"Why didn't you?" said Maggie. "After we were gone, when they waited for him to come back for his things, and still he didn't come?"

"Why should I? What would have been the good? What did I care about his things? Could I have brought him back from the dead by telling?"

"You are quite sure, then—you were quite sure all the time—that he *is* dead?"

It was the only question that remained, whether she asked it of herself or Friedl.

"His body," she said, "never came ashore. I don't say that is proof of anything, I only say it is so. If there is anything more that you know, anything final, please tell me."

There was a soundless movement in the dark, and Friedl's

face was close to hers, pale and fierce beneath the black hair.

"Dead?" she said softly. "Yes, he's dead. You are right, I didn't tell your Herr Killian everything I know. The body never came ashore here in Austria, no—*but in Germany it did*! That same winter they sent me over to help at the hotel in Felsenbach. Marianne is married to the innkeeper there, and they have a good ski season while we are quiet here. You do not know this place? Our river runs through it after it leaves the lake, before it comes back into Austria. That year there was a sudden thaw early in February, and the Rulenbach came down out of the lake in flood and brought a man ashore. What was left of a man! No, I still did not speak! Why speak? What could it do for him or for me? And after so long one would not say he was recognisable, no, not easily recognisable. He had no papers on him . . . how could he? Almost he had no clothes. They buried him out of charity, and put a stone over him, too, but without a name. But *I* knew!" she cried, her voice rising dangerously. "*I* knew who he was! You want proof? He still had a signet ring on his finger, after all that time. I saw it, and I knew it. And so will you know it! Don't take my word, look for yourself! Do you remember *this*?"

The pale claw of her hand plunged suddenly into the pocket of her dress, and plucked out a slip of white card, and something else that she fumbled wildly for a moment before her shaking fingers could control it. She had come prepared with everything she needed for the *coup de grâce*. The torch was a tiny thing that nestled in her palm, but it produced a thin bright beam, enough for her purpose.

"Look! *Look!* You wished to know—*know*, then, be certain! Do you remember this face?"

She thrust it before Maggie's eyes, and held the torch-beam close. A postcard photograph, half-length, of a young man playing the 'cello. It was taken somewhat from his right side; his head was inclined in delighted concentration over his instrument, so that the eyes were veiled beneath rounded lids, and the highlight picked out the line of a smooth boyish forehead and a well-shaped jaw and chin. The lips, full and firm, curled slightly in an absorbed smile, the hair, wavy and thick, was shaken forward out of its concert-platform neatness by his exertions. He looked young, carefree, and as single-minded as a child. And the photographer, like every photographer who ever made studies of a string-player, had lavished his most loving care on the braced and sensitive hands. The bow hand, beautiful in its taut grace and power, occupied the forefront of the picture; and on the third finger was a heavy seal-ring with a black, oval stone. Even by this light Maggie could distinguish the curling flourishes of the letter R in reverse.

"Can you see clearly enough? Here, take it, hold it . . . It was you he wanted . . . you who killed him. Yes, killed him! Is it the right man? Is it the right ring? You know him?"

"Yes," said Maggie in a broken whisper. "Yes, I know him."

Friedl snatched away her hand, and left the photograph quivering in Maggie's hold. She had reached the end of the journey, there was nowhere beyond to go. The darkness and the watery shimmer, the pencil of torch-light, the pale glare of Friedl's vengeful face, lurched and swirled round her in a moment of faintness, and suddenly the burden of this corrosive hate was more than she could bear. Her last refuge was gone, she could no longer hold on to any shred of doubt or hope. The photograph fluttered from her nerveless fingers. She turned and stumbled away through the bushes, blind and desperate, fending herself off from trees, tripping over roots, wild to escape from contact with this malice that pursued her with a defilement worse than guilt. Behind her she heard Friedl break into hard, breathless laughter, and swoop through the bushes to follow her victim still.

"Run . . . faster, faster . . . He is on your heels!"

Tearlessly sobbing, half-demented, Maggie clawed her way out to the open path at last, and began to run unsteadily along it, her course wavering from one grassy edge to the other, her hands spread to ward off the leaning trees. Once she fell, and picked herself up with wincing haste and blundered on. The voice had fallen far behind now, abandoning her to her own torments. No sound pursued her. She halted for a moment, clinging to the resinous trunk of a fir tree in the fragrant darkness, her chest labouring, her ears straining, awed and soothed by the night's huge silence.

It was then that she heard the sound. Not loud, if the measure of the preceding silence had not newly alerted her spirit, not even significant, if it had been the first time she had heard it. But this was time returning, experience rounding on itself to celebrate her destruction. This she had heard before, a long time ago, and pushed away from her strenuously into the limbo of disbelief because it must not be true. Some way behind her, distantly but clearly, echoed the mute, remembered splash of a body into water. She was mad, or damned, or both, she was the quarry of a specific retribution. History had dragged back a September night of many years ago, so that she should not be able to forget, or find it possible to mistake her hour.

When she could breathe again she crept on, mindless, exhausted, sunk now into the indifference of despair. The comfortable brown bulk of the hotel rose before her out of the trees. She dragged herself up the wooden steps to her own verandah, and let herself in by the curtained door. The furies were hard on her heels, but she could not run any more, and it was not from them she was in flight. Without putting on the light she fell face-upwards on her bed, and lay with spread arms, staring up at the high ceiling, waiting to embrace the judgment.

She knew, she acknowledged, her mortal guilt. A fellow-creature had leaned upon her in his extreme need, and she had shrugged him off and let him fall. She admitted to her consciousness at last the truth of what she was. She was Robin Aylwin's murderess.

*

She was roused from her timeless, aimless waiting before the first light of dawn had turned the sky from velvet black to smoke-grey. Something was pecking irritably at her senses, a small, insistent, nagging thing that hurt, and meant to hurt. With infinite labour her mind gathered its abandoned powers to locate and understand. Someone was tapping, tapping, softly and tirelessly at the glass of the door in her sitting-room, the door that led to the verandah and the lake.

She rose like a sleepwalker, and felt her way across the bedroom. All the shapes within the room were defined in shades of grey. The sky framed in the window was metallic and bluish, like steel, and the outline of the figure pressed into the angle of the door-frame was black, sexless, without identity, one edge of it merged into the wall. Only the hand that tapped and tapped at the glass with some small hard object had a perceptible shape and size. A man's hand, tapping out that minute but penetrating sound with his keys to wake her.

She had no thoughts, no curiosity, and no fear. She drew back the bolt. The cool of the outer air gushed in before him as he slid into the room quickly and silently, and closed the door behind him. Her hand had gone up automatically to the light switch, but he caught her by the wrist before she could reach it.

"No, don't! No lights! They'd see them."

She passed a hand confusedly over her eyes, for she was surely seeing and hearing things that could have no reality. The voice she knew, and the face, so close to her own in the dimness. Even the hard grip of the hand holding her was familiar. If he had not been many miles away in England, she would have said this was Francis Killian in the flesh, so solid did the apparition seem. She stood passive, not trying to free herself, not even recoiling from being handled, from having her haunted solitude trampled, from having to experience at close quarters his love and rage and fear for her. The force that frowned off the world to a respectful distance had deserted her and left her a shell.

He stood from between her and the paling light from outside, and turned her about in his hands, saw the grass-stains on her skirt, the torn stockings, the deep bruises under her eyes. He took her by the chin and turned her face up to him with a groan of exasperation.

"My God, my God, what have you done?" he said, hardly audibly, but that was to himself, not to her. "Oh, God, why did I ever take my eyes off you? Even at night! I thought you were safe in your bed . . ."

"It *is* you!" she said, with distant wonder. "How did you get here?"

"I followed you. Did you think I could just wash my hands of you and let you go to hell alone? Why, for God's sake," he demanded, his enforced whisper shaken and thick with fury, "did you have to do this crazy thing? Couldn't you trust me and take my word for it? Why did you have to come here and expose yourself to *this*? And what were your damned fools of doctors doing to let you?"

She had nothing to say. He held her by the shoulders and she stood silent and submissive, looking at him, looking through him, with eyes huge and dulled, as though she still dreamed of him and had no interest in waking. Her passivity terrified him. He shook her between his hands, too frightened to be gentle.

"Don't you understand? Don't you realise your position? Don't you know that Friedl never came in last night? *That they've just fished her body out of the lake?*"

CHAPTER VII

SOMETHING came to life again in the dull depths of her eyes, a quivering intelligence that proved she was still within reach of argument and persuasion, if only he had had time for either. But it was growing lighter every moment, and he had to get out of there quickly, or she would have no chance at all. There was no time to question her. He made one attempt, and she said nothing, merely stood withdrawn into some remote dream of horror. There was nothing he could do but take charge of her, and hope to God she would do what he told her, and be too numbed to realise what a tightrope she was walking until she was safely over.

He drew her across the room in his arm, and thrust her into her bedroom.

"Get those clothes off, quickly! Give me the stockings and the dress . . . Hurry, I'll get them out of here."

She went where he urged her and did what she was told like an automaton. In a few moments she emerged in her housecoat, the torn stockings and stained dress in her hands. He bundled them into his pockets, and drew her to the bed, and sitting her down there, held her by the shoulders eye to eye with him.

"Listen to me! The police will be here all day, asking questions of everybody. You, too! You've got to be ready for them. *You know nothing about Friedl*, you understand? You didn't see her last night, you weren't with her . . ."

It was then that her face awoke suddenly, stirred into agitation and pain, for it was then that it dawned on her that he half-believed she had killed Friedl. And in a sense so she had. There was a doom on her. People who came too near her died, without any motion of her will. And so might he, if she did not send him away from her.

"I must tell you," she said, raising upon him eyes no longer blind, but brilliant with apprehension and resolve. "I did see her . . . I was with her . . ."

"I've asked you nothing," he said roughly. "I don't want to know."

"*I want to tell you*. There was more, something she didn't tell you . . ."

"Quickly, then!" He eyed the paling light, and shook with anxiety for her.

She had caught the sting of his urgency at last. She told him what she had to tell in a few words. He held fast to her all the while, afraid that she might relapse into her border world of despair if he took his hands from her.

"Felsenbach! That's over in the Allgäu. And this photo-graph . . . you're in no doubt that it is Aylwin?"

She shook her head. "It's Robin. There isn't any doubt."

"You went out by the varandah here . . . No one saw you? No one was about, when you left or when you returned?"

"No, no one."

"Good, that makes it easier. If people saw you come upstairs after dinner, so much the better. Understand, you went to bed, and you've been here ever since. You've been ill, you're under orders to get plenty of rest." They'll believe that, he thought, his heart aching over the pale spectre he held between his hands. "You understand? You went early to bed, and slept, and you know nothing about any happenings in the night. That's what you have to tell the police, when they ask, and for God's sake get it right and stick to it."

"I won't forget," she said submissively.

"And listen, stay close to the hotel all to-day. Maybe they'll insist on that, but do it in any case. But to-morrow come to the restaurant in the village, for lunch, and I'll meet you there. The one next to the church, The Bear. Make it about noon. By then we may be able to see how the land lies. We're acquaintances in England, running into each other here by chance. Have you got that clear?"

In a whisper she said: "Yes," and let it be taken for a promise, though she had promised nothing. All she wanted now was for him to go away quickly, before the shadow fell upon him as it had fallen on Robin and on Friedl.

"I must get out of here, it'll be broad daylight soon. When I've gone, go to bed, sleep if you can, but go to bed anyhow, and when it's time, get up and go down to breakfast as if nothing had happened. As far as you're concerned, *nothing has happened*! That's all you have to remember."

He left her there sitting on the edge of her bed, looking after him. Soundlessly he turned the latch of the door, and silently let it relax into its place again under his hand. The pre-dawn light was now dove-grey, but the woodland below, the invisible shore, the gardens, still drowsed in obscurity and silence. Quicksilver, dully shining, the lake lay in its bowl asleep; when the sun rose there would be faint curls of mist drifting across its surface on the south-west wind. Towards the north-east, and the dwindling corner where the Rulenbach flowed out on its detour across the German border. Towards Felsenbach, where, if Friedl had been telling the truth, Robin Aylwin was buried in a grave without a name.

*

When he was gone, she did as he had told her to do. She went to bed, and by some curious process of subconscious obedience she even fell asleep. She slept until the sun was high, and the usual morning noises had come to life all round her, the normal echoes of an old, spacious house with bare wooden floors. She rose and dressed herself with care, and made up her face as scrupulously as for a stage performance, which in a way this day was going to be.

She went down the stairs slowly, straining her ears at every step. There was a changed quality in the bustle of sound within the house, a high, soft, hysterical note on tension. From the staircase windows that looked into the courtyard she saw a police car and an ambulance standing on the cobbles. Within the broad double doorway of the hall Herr Waldmeister stood conversing earnestly and in low tones with a middle-aged police officer. Frau Waldmeister, in the doorway of the office, talked volubly to someone within, in a cataract of excited dialect supplemented with a frenzy of shoulder-heaving and head-wagging, and when Maggie passed by she could see another, younger policeman busy clearing the office desk for his own use. Two or three guests hovered just within the doorway of the dining-room, peering and whispering in delighted horror.

Gisela, hunched over her adding machine, punched out figures blindly with one hand, and held a handkerchief to her nose with the other. Not to question or comment would in itself be ground for comment. Maggie turned towards the reception desk.

"Whatever's the matter? What is it? Has something happened?"

Gisela looked up with brimming eyes. "Oh, Miss Tressider, isn't it terrible? The police are here, they want to talk to everybody. Friedl . . . she's dead! She drowned herself in the lake!"

*

It was late in the afternoon before the police got round to Maggie. By then it was quite simply a relief to be called into the office, and it seemed to her that in closing the door behind her on entering she shut herself into a quiet island, immune to all the agitation and gossip and rumours that were convulsing the household. There was excitement, disquiet and awe abroad in the Goldener Hirsch; but there was no grief. Only Gisela, in love with living and genuinely sorry that anyone should have to surrender it, much less feel wretched enough to want to opt out of it, had shed tears.

In the office it was very quiet. The young man behind the desk, thickset, solid and tanned, looked up from the list he had before him, and smiled briefly and perfunctorily in tribute to a good-looking woman. Off-duty, he would have had more time to appreciate her.

"Sit down, please. You are Miss Maggie Tressider?"

"Yes," she said, "that's my name."

"And you occupy room Number One. You know what our business is here?"

"Gisela told me, this morning. One of the maids has been drowned in the lake."

"Friedl Schiffer . . . yes. We took her body from the water very early this morning." He did not say what had brought them looking for her there at such an hour, but the rumours were already circulating, and by this time there were not many people in Scheidenau who did not know that a celebrated local poacher, out before daylight after his night-lines, had sighted the body in the water and given the alarm. "Did you know her well?"

"I've been here only two days," said Maggie simply. "I knew her by name and by sight, of course, I've talked to her once or twice, but that's all."

"We are anxious to find out when she was last seen alive.

Can you help us? When was the last time that you saw her?"

"She helped to serve dinner. After that I didn't see her again. I went up to bed very shortly afterwards." She caught his shrewd brown eye on her, and smiled faintly. "I am not exactly on holiday. About a month ago I was involved in a car crash, and had some rather troublesome but not dangerous injuries, which required surgery. I came here for a complete change and rest during convalescence."

He nodded sympathy; it had already dawned on her that he knew quite well who Maggie Tressider was, and in spite of all his professional impartiality he would find it very easy to treat her as a privileged person. It made her almost ashamed of pleading illness, however truthfully. "I am almost well," she said quickly, "only not yet quite strong again."

"May I say that I hope this tragedy will not upset you too much? You must try to put it out of your mind once this enquiry is over, and I trust the air of Scheidenau will restore you to health. We are hoping to have the pleasure of hearing you at Salzburg again next year." He turned back to the business in hand without hesitation and without embarrassment. "Your room is on the lake side of the house. Did you hear or see anything out of the way? During the evening or in the night?"

"No. I have sleeping tablets," she said apologetically. It was not even a lie; she had them, though she never took them. They were the doctors' idea, not hers. "When I came down this morning you were already here, and Gisela told me what had happened."

It seemed that he was satisfied; he was marking off her name in his list. "One more thing. I would like you to look at this."

He took it from under the papers on the desk; she knew it as soon as her eyes lit upon it, and it went to her heart like an invisible arrow, reminding her that she was herself the instrument not of one death only, but of two. She put out a hand that astonished her by not trembling—perhaps there was nothing left to make her tremble, if she accepted that sentence of damnation—to take the photograph he was offering her. She bent her head over it dutifully, and the passion with which she studied it was no lie.

It was the one thing for which she had not been prepared, and for a moment she did not know what to do. The boy in the photograph, head bent like hers, brow furrowed like hers, braced hands fleetingly happy in making music, bowed away at his 'cello and ignored her. No one could have cared less what she did about him; that was her affair. A stain of damp from the dewy grass had dried across one corner, a smear of green marked the neck of the 'cello. Suddenly she wanted with all her heart to acknowledge this boy, to declare her interest in him and her grief for him, and above all her endless and inescapable responsibility for his death. But she could not do it. If she dealt herself in, how long would it be before Francis Killian was dragged in beside her?

She shook her head helplessly, and looked up at the man behind the desk. "Who is he? Is it something to do with Friedl?"

"We should be interested to have him identified. Do you know him?"

So all the Waldmeister family had either genuinely not remembered Robin Aylwin, or else preferred not to know him, not to be drawn in any deeper. She wondered which? "No," she said, "I don't know him."

"You never saw this before?"

"I'm sorry!" That at least was no lie; she was sorry that she could not lay down the load that was again crushing her, but if she did, someone else would find himself carrying it.

"Thank you, Miss Tressider, that is all. Don't worry, we shall try not to disturb you any more. Rest and relax, and think about other things."

"You're very kind," she said, and meant it. At the door she hesitated, looking back. It was without premeditation that she asked: "Did Friedl fall in? Or . . . do you think she did it herself?"

She was never quite sure, afterwards, why he answered her, and apparently so unguardedly. Perhaps the directness of the question had surprised an answer out of him before he was aware; but that she could hardly believe. Or perhaps it was a deliberate concession on his part to a person he held to be above suspicion. She hoped it was not that. Or perhaps, and most probably of all, he chose her to fly a little kite for him, to put a small and deceptively innocent cat among the pigeons, in order to see what birds, if any, took flight, and what feathers flew.

"Hardly either," he said with a hollow smile, "if the fingermarks round her throat mean anything. Goodday, Miss Tressider!"

*

She walked out of the office and up the staircase like a creature in a dream. She saw no one, she heard nothing but that matter-of-fact voice repeating its calculated, its miraculous indiscretion. A huge, clean, boisterous wind was blowing through her mind and spirit, blowing the sickness from her soul and the corruption from her will. She closed the door of her room, and sat down before the mirror to stare into her own face, and saw it marvellously changed. She felt cold and pure, scoured into her ultimate clarity, like a Himalayan peak honed diamond-clear and diamond-hard by the withering winds of the heights. She saw herself bright and positive and brave in the mirror, and wondered where this self of hers had been hiding so long.

He would never know what he had done for her!

Friedl had died in the lake, but with the marks of hands round her throat. That meant murder! Not the obscure, malign influence of a woman who was accursed and carried death around with her against her will, but simple, physical, brutal murder, ordered by a human brain and carried out by two human hands. Not her hands, and not her brain. She was absolved; this at least she *knew* she had not done, nor caused to be done. Someone else had been prowling the woods at midnight, spying on them. A dead twig had cracked underfoot, and Friedl had shrugged it away as of no significance. And if this was plain, workaday murder, then surely so had Robin's death been, long ago.

Not hers at all, never hers, neither the act nor the guilt. All she had been was the diversion, the instrument, the fool of God blundering about helplessly in the path of some other force not troubled with a conscience.

There was someone else, then, who had wanted Friedl dead. There was someone else who had wanted Robin dead. What a fool she had been, what an inflated fool, thinking herself so important that heaven would put itself out to spread its lightnings round her! Humility came to her aid now, she saw herself small and accidental, ridiculously irrelevant. Some other more urgent, more practical reason must account for these deaths. Someone else's advantage, or profit, or threatened security.

So *why*? Why kill Robin? Why kill Friedl? These two deaths, however far divided in time, could not be separate. There was no possibility of mere coincidence. Friedl had lived safely enough here all those years, but she had not long survived once she began to answer questions on this one subject. Questions which it seemed had never been asked by anyone before. She was malevolent and talkative, and she died. Someone had reason to fear her tongue. Someone who knew all about Robin Aylwin's death. Someone who flourished in anonymity and did not wish to be investigated, someone who could not permit curiosity, who could not *afford* curiosity!

The more she considered what knowledge she had, the more certain did it seem to her that the murderer of Robin and the murderer of Friedl Schiffer were one and the same. Why else should it be necessary to stop Friedl's mouth?

It seems, she told the bright, transfigured self in her glass, that these things began happening because I began to probe Robin's disappearance. His death, though I didn't know that at the time, not for certain. So that gives us all the more reason for continuing to probe, but also all the more reason for doing it very, very carefully, and thinking out and covering up every move before we make it. Above all, for going over every single word either of us got out of Friedl. Because she must have told us more than we've realised yet, if only we can find out which bits are really significant.

To-morrow, she promised herself, I shall have help. Over lunch I'll tell him all this, he'll know how to go on from there, what we ought to do. Go straight to the police and tell them all we know and all we guess, or hold back until we have more to offer? I've already lied, I can bear to stay a liar until then, because he's implicated, too, once I admit what I know about last night. I can make no move until I've seen him.

So that was settled, and she was left staring in delight and disbelief at that shining image before her, with gentian eyes dilated and radiant, and a soft flush of excitement like summer bloom on her pale cheeks. She thought, astonished: He's never really seen me, and I've never really seen him. We shall be meeting for the first time!

*

At about the same hour of the afternoon when Maggie celebrated her miraculous restoration to sanity and health by washing her hair and giving her favourite dress to a chambermaid to be pressed, Francis Killian was standing beside a grave in the small cemetery of Felsenbach, five miles inside the German frontier.

A little excursion over the border into the Allgäu, itself a very charming district and on terms of intimate exchange with its southern neighbours, is a normal enough way of spending a day if you happen to be a tourist in the northern Vorarlberg or the north-western Tirol. And since English tourists habitually visit churches, even those tourists who hardly ever enter a church at home, Francis had felt it to be natural enough to make for the churchyard and do his own hunting, rather than risk asking leading questions in any of the inns of Felsenbach, let alone the one which belonged to the husband of Marianne Waldmeister. Buried, Friedl had

said, as a charity, and with a stone over him, but without a
name. That should be data enough to identify what Francis
was looking for. If there was a stone there would be some
inscription on it, if only to call attention to the piety of the
donor.

Felsenbach lay in a shallow bowl among the hills, with the
river circling round it, one bank deeply undercut. In the
spring thaw this insignificant little stream would come down
fast and bring a great deal of the débris of the higher lands
with it. Now in the moist, mild September weather the
Rulenbach ran lamblike round the northern edge of the
village, and threatened no one.

The church lay on the southern fringe of the village, on
rising ground, and the cemetery spread over a gentle plateau
behind it. An old church, squat, whitewashed, with an onion
cupola weathered to a beautiful Indian red. Its thick walls
had a heavy batter, its windows were small and sunk far into
the masonry like deep-set eyes. The burial ground, too, was
old and thickly populated. Francis saw confronting him a
miniature forest of close-planted, rigid little trees, wooden-
shafted trees with complicated foliage of iron filigree and
paper blossoms, and violet mourning ribbons turning a
uniform dun-colour with age and weather.

He made several exposures of the church, in case anyone
was interested in his activities, though it seemed unlikely,
and one of the valley from over the tiled crest of the
boundary wall; and then he began to move among the
graves, taking a picture here and there. The display of iron-
work was fantastic enough to turn any addict camera-happy.
Most of the older memorials, the carved wooden crosses and
pale stone kerbs, bore framed photographs of the dead, some
of them so worn and faded that only a feature or two survived, a vast moustache from early in the century, a pair of
unwavering, sad eyes, a piled nest of frizzy hair. Some of the
newer granite headstones had their frontal surfaces glazed
black, to carry more permanent and more startling reminders
of the people they commemorated, portraits engraved into

the glaze to last as long as the stone. These were never going to mellow into anonymity, every rain washed them clean, even if every All Souls' Day had not turned out the survivors with detergent and chamois leather to make sure not a line was lost.

It took him an hour or more to find the one he was looking for, but once found there was no mistaking it. It was tucked into a far corner of the cemetery, close to the waste plot where old flowers and garlands were piled together to await destruction, and it was the only stone he saw which was both modern and neglected. The charity which had buried Robin Aylwin could not be expected to visit him annually and clean him up for the festival of the dead; and even if the church took care of this task, the grave had had almost a year now to get overgrown. The grass was roughly trimmed back from it, there was still one faded wreath, but the black mirror of the squat headstone was filmed here and there with a thin layer of grey lichen. Nevertheless, its most startling aspect was immediately apparent; above the inscription there was an engraving of what was certainly a human head.

Francis found himself a fine sliver of shale, and began to pare away the growth of lichen, and then with a handful of moist paper flowers from the waste heap scrubbed the surface clean. The thing sprang out at him unnervingly clear and improbable. It was a human head, certainly, and with enough individuality in the face to suggest a portrait; but it differed from all the rest in being recumbent and seen in half-face, as you might have seen it if you had been called to identify it on a slab in the morgue. The eyelids were closed, the young features frozen into the lofty detachment of death. The thick hair, streaming back from the bland forehead as if still heavy with the water of the Scheidenauersee, had yet a suggestion of waves in it. The lips, full and firm, curled a little at the corners with a suggestion of the self-confidence of life. In its way it was an impressive piece, a pious generalisation for drowned youth, and yet with a markedly individual personality of its own.

Which, of course, was absurd! *Or was it?* Granted the corpse must have been at least four months in the water before it came ashore, they had been the winter months of almost total frost. Even if the clothes had been a complete loss, as Friedl had said, the body might still have retained some indications of its living appearance, enough to guide a skilled man. The doctor who conducted the post-mortem might even have advised on a reconstruction from the bones of the face. Given the interest, it could be done. But would the result look like this? Or perhaps it was entirely fanciful; the romantic and morbid German temperament, Francis reflected, had done stranger things than this in its time. And perhaps some rich man not far from the end of his span was concerned rather with making his own soul than salvaging Robin Aylwin's. The elaboration of his offering was what mattered.

Beneath the portrait—for reconstructed or imaginary, it was a portrait—was an inscription in German. Francis translated it loosely, and wondered:

> "Pray for the repose of an unknown young man, drowned in the Rulenbach, and for those who erected this memorial over him.
>
> February 1956."

A modest donor, he had left his own name out of it along with the necessary omission of the victim's. Francis used up the rest of his film on the grave. The light was still good, and the definition in the engraving excellent. Developing the results would not be so easy, but at this time of year the backlog of work in the local studio would not be great, and a little persuasion and a discreet bribe might get him his pictures by to-morrow morning if he hurried back and handed over the film now. He would have preferred to spend a little time in making friends with the photographer and getting him to lend his darkroom, but with a police investigation going on in Scheidenau even so small a departure from the norm would invite attention. No, better just be a tourist in a hurry, there was nothing abnormal about that.

He went to the trouble, before he departed, to inspect every face of the stone. There was something about it that made him uneasy, something small and prosaic in which it differed from its kind, quite apart from the macabre quality of the work involved; but for the life of him he could not put his finger on it.

He picked up his car in the square, and drove back through the valley towards Austria. For two or three miles the road was a gentle rise with open meadow views. Then, in the belt of country near the frontier, there were broken woodlands and outcrop rocks, and more than one short but dramatic defile between high walls of forest and cliff. In this complex countryside echoes played strange tricks. Occasionally he would have sworn that he was about to meet another car, yet nothing appeared, and it seemed that the sound of his own engine was being flung back to him from some oblique face of rock ahead. Twice he thought he caught the note of a car following him, and once went so far as to cut his engine and slide in among the trees to see if anything passed by; but nothing did, and as soon as the note of his own motor ceased he was surrounded by a profound silence. It was a dark, enclosed road, little frequented at this time of year. He completed the ascent, and emerged into the comparative daylight of the westward side, winding down among rolling meadows to the Customs' barrier. A bored official urged him through. In twenty minutes he was passing the Alte Post and entering Scheidenau.

*

In the darkness under the trees he stood and watched her windows, but he went no nearer than the water's edge, where the public path in the little park ended; for she was there, safe. he need not wonder about her to-night.

She was singing. The notes of the piano prelude drifted across the lambent silver of the water, refined into unearthly purity and clarity. And then the voice, molten gold, pouring out on the air a passion of hope and longing.

"Die Welt wird schöner mit jedem Tag,
Man weiss nicht, was noch werden mag,
Das Blühen will nicht enden . . ."

Walled in and overshadowed with autumn, murder and sorrow, she sang about spring and hope and certainty, proclaimed that the world grew more beautiful every day, that no one could guess what miracle would happen next, what prodigy of blossom burst before a man's eyes. And you would have thought, he reflected with an aching heart, that she truly believed it, she in her sickness and loneliness and undefined danger. Such a demon she had in her, and so little did it consider her. If he had not known in what extremity he had unwillingly left her that morning, he would have said, yes, this is the acme of joy.

"Es blüht das fernste, tiefste Tal.
Nun, armes Herz, vergiss der Qual!
Nun müss sich alles, alles wenden,
Nun müss sich alles, alles wenden."

Now, poor heart, forget your pain; Now everything, everything must change!

I wish, he thought, following the last droplet of the postlude to its silvery resolution far over the lake, I wish I believed it. For you it may yet, my beautiful, my darling, for you it shall if I can make it. But not for me.

CHAPTER VIII

MAGGIE pushed open the door of the restaurant Zum Bären just ten minutes after noon. He was there before her, credibly installed alone at one of the smaller tables for two. He saw her come, and his face, after the first blank glance, lit up with what she took for a creditable impersonation of a rather bored tourist spotting a totally unexpected acquaintance, though in fact the bravery of her appearance and the bloom that awakening had cast over her pallor and frailty had dazzled him out of all pretence. Maggie had been right, he was seeing her for the first time; the trouble was that he did not realise it. What he believed he was seeing, blessedly reassuring and agonisingly lovely though he found it, was what she could do by way of putting on a show when her life and future were at stake. Even so, he marvelled and adored her for it; but he would have been very chary indeed of taking it as genuine.

She walked across the room between the tables with her head up and her eyes roving, and her stride was young and elastic and easy, it would have done for the self-confident débutante she had never been. She made to pass him, and then looked straight at him, and halted, swinging upon him with delighted face and eagerly outstretched hand.

"Mr. Killian! Well, what are *you* doing here? How nice to see you!"

Not overdone, either, he thought with rueful approval; the voice still subdued, meant only for him, even the gesture preserving a thoroughly English restraint. She was, after all, an experienced opera singer, and no one needs acting skill more.

It was at that moment that he observed the man who had entered so unobtrusively after her. A tall man in a grey suit, who was just hanging up his hat and taking a seat at a table not too close to them, but strategically placed beside a pillar faced on its six sides with mirrors. He had his back to them, and the table was so aligned that Francis could not even see his face in the mirrors, but the stranger had only to turn his head a little to keep a close eye on them.

On his feet, beaming painfully at the apparition of beauty that was not and never could be his, going through the motions of inviting her to join him, seating her devotedly, Francis said into her ear, with no change of expression or intonation: "You've picked up a shadow. No, don't look round! He's several yards away, he can't hear us if we're careful, but he has us under observation. Keep acting, and slip in what you want to say among the chatter."

He felt her stiffen for an instant, but when he sat down opposite her she was smiling at him. "How wonderful to meet somebody to whom I can talk in English. My German has been strained to the limit. Police, do you mean?"

"Yes, plain clothes. Very discreet. But for the hat I'd have said English." He handed her the menu. "Tell me what you're doing here?"

Frowning over a plethora of dishes, she said, "Convalescing. But it seems I may have picked the wrong place. You'll have heard about our excitement? They were easily satisfied, it went all right. I got something, too, something definite." She looked up at him over the long card with its border of vine-leaves. "You think the venison would be a good idea?"

"I think it might. Beer or wine?"

"Wine. You choose." She leaned her elbows on the table and cupped her chin in her hands. It brought her a little nearer to him, and made it possible to use her fingers to screen the movement of her lips. *"Friedl was murdered. He told me there were fingermarks round her throat."*

Francis kept the easy social smile fixed on his face; he had to, the man by the mirrors had just shifted his chair very slightly to have them more favourably in view.

"There's an open red wine, a local, shall we try it? *The police told you that?"*

"Yes. All right, let's." She sat back as the waiter approached to take their order. This was not the interview to which she had looked forward. The very smile she was obliged to wear was becoming cramped and painful. Between trivialities they might manage to convey the bare bones of what they had to say to each other, but she would be no nearer knowing whether he believed her, nor could this kind of exchange ever communicate what she felt, the extraordinary sense of deliverance, the revealing quality of the light now that the shadow of guilt had dissolved from

over her. This was the first meeting with him to which she had ever come with an open heart, willing to let him in to her, and because of the stranger watching them they must still remain apart. But she tried. As soon as the soup was served and the waiter had left them she lifted to his face one clear, unsmiling glance. "*I'm cured*," she said.

If he had understood, he made no sign. To talk under these circumstances, in the sense of using language in order to effect a communion between two people, was impossible, and he was not going to attempt it. All they could do was exchange information. Some day there would be a time for doing more than that, but not now. "She was strangled?"

"He didn't say that. Just that there were fingermarks on her throat. Apart from that there's been nothing. I'm just staying in and having a thoroughly lazy time. How about you? Have you got a car here?"

"I hired one in Zurich. Had it waiting for me at the airport." He busied himself with refilling her glass until the waiter had served their venison and left them to enjoy it.

"And have you found anywhere interesting to visit round here?"

"I was over in Germany yesterday," he said. "I went over to look up an old acquaintance, as a matter of fact. In Felsenbach." Obliquely he told her the bare facts of his find, scattered along the way on a verbal conducted tour of one corner of the Allgäu.

"You must show me your pictures some time," she said.

"You may not like them. It could be said I choose rather offbeat targets." He had the sharpest and best of the prints already folded into the menu. "Would you like something to follow?" He held out the card to her across the table, open, the blown-up photograph carefully secured by a forefinger. "See what you think."

Her eyes lit upon the starkly outlined face just before her fingers touched, and for an instant the colour was shocked out of her cheeks. Her mask shook, and was resolutely clamped back into place. She took the menu from him, and sat steadily gazing at the print.

"Yes, I think so. *Yes . . .*"

"An idealised guess?"

"*A likeness*. The way the eyes are set . . . *and the mouth
. . .*" But for Friedl's thirteen-year-old treasure it might have
been hard for her to recall that exact curl of the lips.
"Formalised, but really a likeness." In Friedl's picture the
full lids had also covered and hidden the eyes, whose colour
she could not remember, and the lips had borne this same
shadow of a smile. Maggie handed the menu back with
composure. "I'll just have fruit, I think. And coffee."

Francis palmed the print and slipped it back into his
pocket under the table. The setting of the eyes she had
remarked on first; well, that could be guessed at even after
months, better than a guess, in fact. There is nothing much
more durable than bone. But the mouth . . . That was
another matter. The soft tissue of the lips, even if it survived
through the frost, surely would not retain much of its
normal shape after being buffeted downstream in the thaw.

Maggie peeled a pear with rather strained attention, and
asked brightly, without looking up: "Have you any plans for
this afternoon?"

"I thought I might have another drive in the same direction. There are some rather good woodcarvers over there, I
might have a look what's to be found. Other artists, too."

"*Take me with you!*" she said.

The first time she had ever asked him for anything except
in return for a fee, and it was the one thing he would not
and could not do for her. He wanted her safe in the Goldener Hirsch, with the police on the premises and a good lock
on the door.

"If I were you I should stay in and get plenty of rest.
With all this disturbance you must have been under a good
deal of strain. Stay in, let them see you're there on call, not
anxious, not involved."

"I suppose it might be a good idea," she admitted.

"Wait for me to-night. I'll come to you as soon as I can.
By the verandah. Then we can talk."

"*Yes!*" she said eagerly. She set down her empty coffee cup, and looked at him for a moment helplessly and hopefully across the table. "*You will come?*"

"I'll come."

"What do we do about getting out of here? You think it's me he wants, or you? Shall we leave together?"

"No, you go first, I want to see if he follows."

"At least we gave him time to eat his lunch," said Maggie, and her fixed and tortured brightness dissolved for a moment into a real, youthful, entrancing smile. What might she not be, he thought, if only he could get her safe out of this with her recovered innocence unspotted?

"All right, you say when!"

He wanted her to sit there for a long time, smiling at him like that, but he had a lot to do before he could come to her room at night by the verandah staircase, and he wanted her watched and guarded while he did it. "When!" he said, and groaned inwardly at seeing her rise. He came to his feet with her, hurried to draw out her chair and help her into her light grey coat. "Don't go out at all," he said into her ear, "not anywhere!"

She marshalled coat and gloves and handbag, made a feminine gesture in the direction of her hair without actually touching it, and held out her hand to him.

"Thank you, Francis, it was a lovely lunch. *I shall look forward to seeing you.*"

She was gone, weaving between the tables with her long, free, recovered stride. He stood for a few moments to watch her go, and then sat down again slowly, and lit a cigarette over the dregs of his coffee. His ears were full of her voice speaking his name for the first time, a stunning music, but full of cruel overtones. Gratitude and kindness can do terrible injuries, with the best intentions. It ought to be enough to be of service to her. It had to be enough, there wasn't going to be anything else for him.

The tall man in the grey suit was paying his bill, and rising at leisure to collect his hat from the stand. It was

nice to have been right about something, at least. He kept his
head negligently turned away as he walked to the door, but
one mirror picked up his image in passing and gave Francis
a glimpse of a thin, faintly whimsical, pensive face, of deep
and generous lines and little flesh, with hair greying at the
temples, and deep-set, quiet eyes.

Not, by any stretch of imagination, an Austrian face. Hat
or no hat, that was an English sportscoat, and an English
countenance.

Now what were the English police doing here in the
Vorarlberg, tramping hard on Maggie Tressider's heels?

*

He fretted about her all the way to Felsenbach. But when
all was considered, she was best and safest in the Goldener
Hirsch, with the Austrian police deployed round her on a
murder hunt. He had no doubt at all of the accuracy of what
she had managed to tell him. Friedl had been, if not
strangled, half-strangled and thrown into the lake. Whatever the eccentricity of Maggie's behaviour, they would not
suspect her of an act like that. A woman may perhaps push
another woman into a lake, but by and large, it is only men
who strangle women. By and large, it is only men who have
the necessary hand-span and the necessary force. No, he
could leave her for a few hours. And after that, their best
course might well be to go together and tell their entire story
to the investigators, and leave the rest to them. For the
more complex this business became, the more certain did
he feel that Maggie was entirely and tragically innocent, a
helpless victim caught into somebody else's schemes only by
her hypersensitive conscience, and by the accident of a car
smash which had shaken her off-balance and put all her
defence mechanisms out of gear.

What was ironical was that only after talking to her had
he had been able to put his finger on the thing that was most
wrong with Robin Aylwin's gravestone. All that gratuitous
anonymity! The victim, of course, couldn't be named, no
one knew, or admitted to knowing, his name. But not only
was the donor also anonymous; most improbable of all,

there was not a name, not an initial, not even a mason's mark, anywhere' on that stone to identify the memorial artist who made it! Unheard-of, for the craftsman in death not to avow his work! A monumental mason is a business-man, a tradesman like other tradesmen, he wants his excellence known.

This one didn't. Why?

*

There was only one monumental mason in Felsenbach, indeed only one mason of any kind, a builder of long establishment who employed none but his own family, the ramifications of which ran into three generations. Grave-stones, kerbs, vaults he took in his patriarchal stride. He remembered the corpse from the Rulenbach, he remembered the funeral; but he had had no part in the business of burial or monument. Some wealthy resident of Regenheim, he recalled, had paid for the interment out of goodness of heart, and the small municipality of Felsenbach had natur-ally raised no objection. No doubt some mason from Regen-heim had been employed to make the memorial, afterwards. The donor would obviously look on his own doorstep.

It was another fifteen miles to Regenheim, an undulat-ing, busy road this time, clear of the mountain slopes. The place, when he arrived there, was no bigger than Felsen-bach, but unmistakably more a town. There was a square almost large enough for aircraft landings, a waste of cobbles populated by a handful of cars. There were four or five cramped streets eddying out of it, overhung by black and white houses, tottering archways and jutting upper stories. There was a sprawl of modern villa-buildings beyond. And it was raining. The place had not got its name for nothing.

He parked the Dodge in the square and set about locating whatever monumental masons the town might hold. It was already evening, he had lost more time than he had bar-gained for in reaching this place. He bought some cigarettes at a solid family shop which was still open, and probably would continue so until ten o'clock provided one of the family happened to be spending the evening at home. The woman who served him was elderly and at leisure, and looked as if she and her forebears had been there since Regenheim's free-city days. If anyone knew where to put a finger on every tradesman in the town, she would.

She was very willing to talk, and showed no surprise at being asked for the local furbishers of graves. There were, she said, only two of any substance. One of them, the oldest established, had his mason's yard behind his own house, and he or one of his sons could always be found there. The other had built himself a new villa out on the edge of the town. She gave copious directions for finding it. Then there was, of course, the Klostermann outfit, still in business, though they had few clients now, that side of the family's trade had been neglected since they went in for road haulage. Indifferently she gave him instructions for finding even this unlikely firm, though her large shrug said that she herself wouldn't consider taking them any of her business.

The head of the old-established house happened to be putting away his pick-up in the corner of the yard. He took out a pair of gold-rimmed glasses to inspect the photographs Francis offered him. No, he had never seen this stone before. If he was curious he did not show it; he had been in the world something like seventy years, and learned to concentrate on his own business, and the discipline had paid him well.

The second one, the dweller in the new villa, was a younger man, a go-ahead type with social ambitions and a look of the townsman about him. The villa was aggressively modern and ostentatious, the wife who opened the door was decorative and well-padded. Francis apologised for calling on them out of the blue and at such an hour, and made it clear at once that he wanted only five minutes of their time. He needed, as it turned out, even less than that.

"Thirteen years ago!" said the man of the house, and shook his head decisively. "That is before we came here to open our business. We are from München, we have been here only seven years. I am sorry!"

Which left only the family Klostermann, of whom the old

woman in the tobacconist's had thought so poorly. It was getting dark by then, so Francis was torn two ways; but he was not going back without having a look at even so dim a possibility. He threaded the outer edge of the town, and turned back towards the square by side streets that lacked both the black and white fascination of the town centre and the green spaciousness of the suburbs, but were merely utilitarian early-twentieth-century, without squalor or distinction. And there, sure enough, was a dark and almost empty window, once designed for display, with nothing left in it now but a dusty imitation-marble urn, and a shelf of granite vases with perforated aluminium flower-holders. Beside it the high wall of a yard ran for some distance, double doors set in it. The upper windows were dark, the house was not lived in. But the paint on the gates was new.

The whole place appeared deserted, and Francis might have gone away and left it at that; but as he was turning back to the car a man came briskly along the pavement from the direction of the square, fitted a key into the lock of the yard doors, and let himself in. A thickset, youngish man in a belted leather jacket and a black beret, with a battered briefcase under his arm. Francis gave him a minute or two, and then followed him in. He had left the heavy door ajar, and his lively footfalls clashed diagonally ahead over the cobbles. In the far corner of the yard, in a one-story building obviously added to the original house, a light sprang up.

All one side of the yard was garage doors, and several lorries and vans stood ranged along another wall. Behind the frosted window of what seemed to be the office the dark shape of the leather-coated young man moved vaguely. In a corner of the yard some relics of the expiring monumental business mouldered gently, synthetic granite kerbing, a half-shaped headstone, a small, drooping angel leaning on a cross.

Francis rapped at the office door and pushed it open before him. The man in the leather jacket swung round from the desk under the window, his briefcase open in one hand, a folder of papers in the other. The movement was silent, alert and surprised, but by no means alarmed. He had a smooth, well-fleshed face, high-coloured and bland, with round-set eyes of a bright and yet opaque black, like coal.

"*Was wünschen Sie?*" His voice was gravelly and deep, with no implications of either welcome or animosity.

"Herr Klostermann?"

No, he was not a Klostermann, it seemed. He relaxed, however, on finding that the late caller was looking for his boss. Francis went through his brief explanation for the third time, and produced his photographs. The young man bent his large head over them, breathing stertorously, and considered them for a few moments with respectful attention. Then he shook his head regretfully.

"I am sorry! I am with Herr Klostermann myself only two years. I drive for him. I came to pick up my delivery schedule for to-morrow. With the memorial business I have nothing to do. I do not know if he made this or not. If you could come to-morrow, he will be here."

"I should like to get in touch with him now," said Francis, "if it's possible. I have to drive back to Scheidenau to-night, and I'd rather not have the same journey again if I can help it."

"I am sorry!" He handed back the pictures, and closed his briefcase with deliberation, his round eyes still black and steady on Francis.

"Would there be records here for 1956?"

"No, no records. It is now chiefly a haulage business, everything else he has at his own house."

"Could I go round there to see him now? It would be a great help to me."

"I think he is not there," said the gravelly voice gently. "Wait, I will call the house for you, and see."

He walked away into the dark corner of the room, and opened a narrow door there. His fingers touched the light switch within, and Francis caught a glimpse of a larger, less austere office, with filing cabinets from floor to ceiling along the visible wall, and some pleasant panelling beyond. Then the door was closed firmly between, and he was alone, free to move noiselessly after, and apply his eye to the minute keyhole, and then his ear to the thin panel of the door. It got him very little. There was a long table just within his vision, and the young man was leaning over it, telephone receiver at his ear, dialling a number; but the room within was larger than it seemed, and nothing more than an indistinguishable murmur reached the listener's ear. There was nothing whatever to make his thumbs prick. The young man had said he would telephone, and he was telephoning. A local number, too, or at least somewhere he could dial and get without delay. And he was already cradling the receiver, better get well away from the door before he reached it.

The door opened peacefully, the young man stood shaking his head sadly on the threshold. Behind him the light went out.

"I am sorry, Mr. Klostermann is at his married daughter's house for the evening. I can tell you how to reach him there, if you care to go? It is a farm, about five kilometres from here. You take the road from the square towards Kempten, then two kilometres on you come to a right-hand fork, the signpost says Maienbach. Follow that road for two kilometres, and on the left is a cart road to the farm. It is not hard to find. I should go and speak with Herr Klostermann there. He will not need records to know his own work."

"No," said Francis, "I don't suppose he will. Thank you! If it's only five kilometres I might as well reach him now, and get it settled."

"If you should have to ask, the name at the farm is Haimhofer."

"Thank you very much!"

"*Bitte!*"

Francis walked purposefully across the yard, pulled the unlocked gates to behind him, got into his car and drove up towards the square with aplomb. Arrived there, he circled right-handed about the central parking space, and passed without a second glance the sign marked: Kempten.

Reasonable or not, his thumbs were pricking almost painfully. He took the road for Felsenbach, and stepped hard on the accelerator as soon as he emerged from the narrow confines of the streets. He was heading back towards Scheidenau as fast as he could go.

*

He was past Felsenbach, half-way to the frontier and immured between encroaching plantations of conifers, before he could be quite certain that he was being followed. There were all yesterday's prickings of uneasiness, all yesterday's minute outward signs, but magnified by the extreme, washed clarity of the air. The rain had scrubbed the atmosphere clean as bone, sounds carried as in an echo-chamber. When he stopped his engine for a moment under the trees on a sharp bend, there was not so much a perceptible sound of an engine following, as the vibration of a motor just cut out, by some hypersensitive perception, to match his. Then the superhuman silence. They were there, not too far behind, not too close on his tail; they knew where he was, and were not anxious to overhaul him, as long as they could hold him at this convenient distance, and be sure of not losing him. He wondered what spot they would choose, where they would elect to close the gap. He wished he carried a gun, but knew it was not his weapon and not his style, and that he would have been useless with it even if he had had one. There are killers and non-killers. Guns don't make them.

He was on the climbing sector now, bend after sharp bend, the margins unfenced and with only shallow ditches, the trees crowding close. Silence all round, apart from his own re-echoing sounds, and darkness but for his own headlights glazing and gilding the embossed trunks of the trees, the inset panels of mirror, the scoured faces of rock. If he craned to look upwards he could not distinguish a line where earth and sky met. It had rained fitfully all the way, and was raining still. The sky was shrouded, there were no stars, and no moon.

There must have been someone watching for him, to make

sure that he took the Kempten road and drove into the trap. Maybe they had lost time in setting out after him when he swung past it and turned towards Austria, but he had been fool enough to mention Scheidenau, and they were on his heels now, he was sure of that. The young man in the leather jacket had loosed the hunt after him with a vengeance, and if he was going to shake it, it would have to be now, on this complex stretch where the echoes would play on both sides, and confuse every issue. He put his foot down hard, and gave the car its head. The bends were well engineered, a joy to drive round, but also blind and deaf, at every swing light and sound cut off together, sharp as the descent of a guillotine.

All his senses were so trained on the threat behind that he was, in any case, curiously vulnerable to any hazards ahead. Anything approaching from Austria was his friend and ally, he had no need to be wary of it. Where there was company on the road there was safety. Who could close on him and attack while neutral headlights were bearing down on the scene?

He swung at speed round a right-handed bend, sharp as a shrew's elbow, and straight into the glare of headlights cut off sharp by the curtain of dark trees. Someone was running along the road towards him, a torch in an extended hand waving him down. He braked sharply and drew in to the right, and the face and the torch plunged to a halt and turned back, running alongside him. On the left of the road headlights leaned drunkenly into the ditch. A panting voice alongside implored him:

"*Bitte . . . bitte, halt! Unfall . . .*"

Somebody else's accident was due to be Francis Killian's salvation. Why not buttonhole the pursuers, too, from safe ambush among the victims, flag them down and send them back to call an ambulance, if necessary, or the police? What an irony! Francis pulled in obediently to the side of the road, half on the bald grass verge, swung open the door and piled out of the car, turning to meet the young man who came panting towards him with the torch. He saw a young, frightened, boyish face, wild with relief, blazing at him wide-open welcome.

Something hit him hard on the back of the head. The lights and darks exploded before him, changed places, merged, blinked out into single and absolute darkness. The ground came up and struck him in the face, scoring his cheek and lips raw. He groped along the grass, and the grains of loam were large as boulders. Dimly his mind pursued logic, argued, reproached him. The enemy were in front, not behind. *Then who was behind?* Someone else, assiduous on his heels, but not the enemy. The enemy were these shadows who had struck him down. *Enemies of the enemy, perhaps?* Leave them a sign! Not far behind, he had wondered when they would close the gap. The fingers of his right hand, hooked deep into his left inside pockets, gouged out the wallet that held his photographs, and spilled it into the lush, overgrown autumn grass in the ditch below him. He prised himself up arduously from the ground, the lighter by that load, his head spinning, and levered himself upright on wavering legs, one arm flailing to ward off the first assault.

They were three, he saw them clearly, even photographed them on some emulsion in his mind, his eyes recording nothing. The image sank in, and left his eyes blind.

Two of the three rushed him, one from either side. The third, the boy with the torch, swerved round him as he swayed to his feet, and plunged on. Francis stiff-armed the first of his attackers half across the road, but the second one was on his back in the same moment, one arm crooked round his neck, dragging him over backwards into the shallow ditch. They rolled confusedly together, the wet grass stinging and cold against their faces.

Francis heard a car door slam and a motor thrum into life, and knew it for the note of his hired Dodge from Zurich. Its lights swung impetuously forward and back, forward and back in the road, cutting yellow swathes out of the darkness as it turned, and then it surged past them and roared away at speed in the direction of Felsenbach. That was the last thing Francis knew. His assailant enveloped him suddenly in both arms, and rolled over beneath him, holding him helpless and exposed for the second blow. This time the man with the cosh made no mistake.

The world exploded in a flash of light, and collapsed into chaotic darkness. Francis slid slowly into the ditch, and lay still.

CHAPTER IX

THE BLANKET OF CLOUD on the heights had ripped into tatters and begun to dissolve away just before the smooth sound of the car ahead, steadily climbing, braked into a protesting whine, and the minor confusion of voices, barely audible, nevertheless made itself felt against the surrounding silence.

"*Now* what?" grunted George, who was driving. He put his foot down, willing to narrow the gap a little; nobody was going to hear them approaching, not until they reached that right-hand bend. They were making too much noise themselves, up there. *They!* Somebody had been waiting for Francis Killian, somebody for whom he wasn't prepared, by all the signs. George wanted to know who. "I'm tired of this," he said aloud, "I'm closing up. Hang on, here we go!"

But there they didn't go, or no farther than the twenty yards or so it took him to brake sharply, swing the wheel, wallow across the ditch where a rough logging track crossed it, and burrow an abrupt and hazardous way in among the trees on their right. For at that instant both he and his passenger had caught the sudden rocketing plunge of the Dodge into gear, the sawing alternations of its lunges fore and aft as it turned, and the triumphant roar as it launched into high speed. Its headlights were slicing round the fringe of the trees as the little black police Volkswagen rocked and waddled to a standstill deep among the firs, and George cut motor and lights and prayed that they had been neither seen nor heard.

The young Austrian detective had the passenger door open before the car was still, and was groping and stumbling his way back the few yards to the road. George, afraid to leave the wheel, clawed his way round to peer intently over the back of the driving seat. The car from Zurich shot by at speed, hurtling back the way it had come a few minutes ago, with enough aggression and bravura in the driving to demonstrate blind that it was driven now by another hand. Somebody crude, young and violent. They had followed Francis Killian yesterday, they knew his touch. George never saw the face behind the wheel, but he knew it was not Francis Killian's face. He began to back his way out, tickling the wheel this way and that, grateful that he had grazed nothing in getting in, and fastidiously sensitive to the hazards in getting out. The Austrian detective came running, clambering back into his place and slamming the door just short of the last tree.

"Not your man . . . young fellow driving . . . Couldn't see any passenger. Which way now?"

"Ahead!" said George, and didn't wait to have his judgment endorsed. They swayed drunkenly out on to the road. George cut the lights to sidelights, and nosed uphill, swinging the wheel for the turn.

There were other headlights, somewhere a hundred yards or so round that hairpin, manœuvring rapidly but gently back and forth in a turn, just as the Dodge had done, but this time in the other direction. Their beams lurched upwards and levelled out, as though the car was just heaving itself clear of the ditch, and then danced forward and back and forward again, and the dwindling arc of their light wheeled, threaded the edge of the trees for an instant, and recoiled as the car came round, leaving the bend in the road darkened. But only for a moment. The moon sailed out from rags of cloud, pouring a wash of pallor down the tall

faces of rock ahead, and bleaching the hunched shoulder of
the bend to the white of bone. George accepted the omen
with aplomb, and switched off his lights altogether. He went
round the curve on faith and moonlight, hugging the dark
side.

The car that had just heaved itself out of the ditch
opposite and turned was drawn up now, somewhat farther
ahead than George had estimated, engine running, wheels
barely turning, close to the grass verge. On the verge itself,
faintly outlined by the roof-light through the open door, one
man was stooping with his arms about the end of a long,
unwieldy bundle, which he was thrusting into the rear seat
of the car. Someone else was already in there ahead of it,
hauling it in. A limp, dead weight, all too recognisable as the
feet were dragged aboard and the door slammed on them.
The inside light blinked off, blinked on again as the front
passenger door opened to let the last man leap aboard,
blinked out once again as the car, broad and powerful,
soared into speed and shot away.

Three to one, counting the man at the wheel; four, taking
into account the young one whose job it was to whip away
the hired Dodge somewhere into Germany, and no doubt
get it a new paint job and a changed registration before
daylight to-morrow. Much chance Francis Killian had had,
George thought grimly, drawing a bead on the receding rear
lights, with his foot flat to the floor and his lights still off.
If they were, as he hoped, still undetected, they might as well
stay that way as long as possible. The road surface, thank
God, wasn't bad at all, and the fitful moonlight made the
edge of the grass show up like a kerb; and there was nothing
meeting them, and at this hour of the night, with luck, there
might be nothing all the way to the crest and the frontier.
The lights ahead would indicate the bends, and give him a
chance to use his sidelights without being spotted. With
luck! With, in fact, a lot more luck than Francis Killian had
had.

At the moment the chief trouble was that the big car in
front was gaining rapidly.

"Mercedes, I think!" yelled the young Austrian in his ear, peering excitedly after the shape ahead. His name was Werner Frankel, and he had been assigned to George as escort and assistant because he had received the whole of his primary education and most of his advanced education in English, as a refugee with his family during and after the war. "We shan't overhaul *him*!"

There was no arguing with that; they would be lucky if they could even keep those diminishing tail-lights in view.

"Any hope of a telephone up here?" asked George, keeping his foot down hard, and his eye on the distant spark.

"Yes, an inn, half a mile ahead. You won't see it, but I'll tell you." They were both thinking on the same lines, and it was pleasing to find that they both knew it, without any waste of words. "Drop me off there, and try to hang on to him."

"Sure? You know these roads better than I do."

"You don't speak German," said Werner unanswerably.

George would have managed to make himself understood somehow, but Werner wouldn't even have to try, and delay was what they could least afford.

"You'll call the German police, too? They might pick up the Dodge before they get it into hiding." Nobody was going to be able to identify it afterwards, that was plain. "And the frontier, in case. Though I doubt if they'll risk the frontier . . . not on the road."

"At night it could be a very nominal check . . . they might. If they try some other way over, it has to be a rough one. You'll have a better chance of staying with him."

"And the other side? What choice of roads?"

"After Scheidenau, it has to be Bregenz or Langen. I'll call both. Pity we weren't near enough to get a number, but a Mercedes in a hurry . . . black or dark blue? . . . I'd say black."

"And the Dodge you know." A cigarette-end in the dark, the sole trace of the Mercedes, vanished round one more bend ahead. George switched on dipped headlights, and made up a little of the lost ground while there was a ridge of rock between them.

"The Dodge I know. Slow round this bend, my inn's on the right. You'll see a track going off uphill."

George saw the pole first, the telephone wire sliding away from the road. He braked to a halt where the climbing path began, and Werner was out like a greyhound. "Good luck!" He waved and darted away into the dark; and George ranged through the Volkswagen's willing gears and set off doggedly after the vanished Mercedes.

And now he was on his own, and any communing he was going to do would be done strictly with himself. But give Werner ten minutes with that telephone, and there would be large numbers of invisible allies turning out to his aid. He could use as many as he could get. The outfit that could plant four men and that kind of car to pick off Francis Killian had plenty of resources at its disposal. The thing began to look promisingly big. Big, thorough, and highly sensitive to any display of curiosity. Now which of those calls Killian had made to-day in Regenheim could have caused Them—whoever *They* were!—to set up this efficient ambush?

No doubt about now Werner would be reeling off the whole list to the German police, and leaving them to do the rest. If he was fast enough they might be able to stop the Dodge in Felsenbach, before some discreet garage doors closed on it somewhere—those double doors in Regenheim, perhaps?—and three or four waiting experts fell on it and transformed everything on it or in it that was transformable, and sent it out again to be palmed off on some innocent sucker the other side of the country. George had known the whole job done inside four hours, even in England, and in comparison with these big boys with the whole of Europe open to them the English were mere amateurs.

And if the car was meant to vanish without trace, ten thousand to one so was Francis Killian. Like anybody else who got too nosy about this complicated corner of Central

Europe, about anonymous graves and mysterious disappearances. Like Robin Aylwin himself? Like Peter Bromwich? Hang on tightly enough to this one, thought George, picking up the distant spark and breathing again, and you may find out what happened to the others.

He wished he knew whether the men in that car knew he was there on their tail. His impression was that they did not, for though they were moving briskly, and had left him well behind, the fact remained that with their power they could have been much farther ahead of him had they wished. It looked as if speed, though important and desirable, was not the first consideration. They wouldn't wish to storm the frontier post as if they were in flight from the law; and if, on the other hand, they intended to evade Customs altogether, perhaps they had to look for a way not familiar to them. The crossing between Scheidenau and Felsenbach was a quiet one at any time, surely practically dead at night; but that might be a mixed blessing. Bored Customs men might take more interest in a car passing through than would those who had a constant stream of traffic. No, George's best bet was that they wouldn't go near the post. There are more ways over any hill frontier than are covered by the authorities.

About a mile to go now to the crest. If they were going to leave the road it must be soon, for the descent on the other side was through much more open country. It seemed that suddenly he was gaining on them a little; he could see the spark of red, obviously round another bend from his stretch of road, proceeding in a diagonal incline to the right, and now decidedly at a more sedate speed. He eased up slowly to hold his distance. Arrival at the point where he had seen the quarry change course gave him a shock, for he had been relying on the Mercedes as a guide, and travelling by mere unreliable moonlight or sidelights, or into the sharp cut-off of dipped headlights, which made progress hazardous and the angles of the road deceptive. So far from swinging to the right here, it turned somewhat to the left. He braked with

his nose on the grass verge, and risked switching his lights
on full beam for an instant. He had slightly overshot the
opening of a narrow, stony track that branched off sharply to
the right.

Where they could go, he could go, with room to spare. He
backed a few yards, and turned into the track after them.
His guess had been accurate, they had no intention of entering Austria by the road.

Now he had to use his lights, he would not have survived
long without them. Luckily the driver of the Mercedes must
also be having to concentrate hard, and the noise they were
making up there would effectively drown out the noise he
was making down here. Once launched on this track there
was only one way to go, for trees and rocks encroached on
it irregularly on either side. The surface was beaten earth,
like any ramblers' path in the mountains, liberally toothed
with outcrop rock and loose stones. In places it was more
like a dried watercourse than a track, and in other places
more like a bog than either, and reinforced with half-peeled
logs laid as a causeway. It climbed steeply, twice negotiating
narrow wooden bridges which George took at a crawl, fore-
warned by the earthquake rumblings his quarry had set up
in crossing. Most of the time he lost sight of the Mercedes
altogether, but from time to time he caught a glimpse of the
rear lights, and knew he was holding his own. Caution, not
haste, was what mattered to them here. He could even have
closed up on them, at some risk, but he was unarmed, and
there were three of them, almost certainly provided with
guns. Much better hang back and remain undetected, as
rather surprisingly he still seemed to be, until he could make
contact with the reinforcements called out by Werner.

He had not the least idea at what point they re-entered
Austria; there was never anything to mark the change. Nor
had he any notion of how far they had come on this travesty
of a road; three miles of strained attention can seem more
like thirty. But it occurred to him suddenly that they had
ceased to climb, and on either side of the belt of trees that

shrouded them he could see the faintly lambent sky, still frayed with broken cloud. Then the descent, which was mercifully more gradual than the ascent had been, but still testing enough. The track, doubling like a coursed hare, tipped them abruptly into a lane enclosed between stone walls, no wider than the way they had come, but at once smoother, an ordinary dirt road that might have led to some isolated farm, and probably did. This in turn brought them at length to a metalled road, fields opening out on either side. George rolled the Volkswagen cautiously up to the turn, and cut his lights.

Now he knew where he was. They were back on the main road, a good mile on the Austrian side of the frontier; and well away to the right, solitary on the open sweep of road, the rear lights of the Mercedes were receding rapidly in the direction of Scheidenau.

On this highway no driver had the right to conclude that he was being followed, however many cars he observed behind him. George switched on his headlights, and set off at full speed in pursuit.

*

They circled Scheidenau by a ring road, and beyond the last lights of the village emerged again on to the steel-dark road that headed towards Bregenz. George had hung back at the turn, and let the Mercedes go ahead far enough to convince the driver he was unmarked. Perhaps he allowed him a little too much rope. It couldn't be long now. There should be either a road-block and a police check, or a patrol cruising this way to meet them, on the look-out for a dark-coloured Mercedes. So George idled contentedly his minute too long.

When he drove out on to the straight stretch along the floor of the valley there were no rear lights anywhere to be seen. He put on a spurt to reassure himself that the quarry was still around, but the night remained vacant, calm and clear. The moon was high, the wind had dropped, the rags of cloud had been fretted away into scattered threads. The road ahead was utterly innocent of traffic going his way; and the first thing he encountered was one more black police Volkswagen, cruising gently along to meet him.

Somewhere between the edge of Scheidenau and this point rather less than a mile along the road, the Mercedes and its crew of three and their kidnapped man had all vanished without trace.

CHAPTER X

EVER SINCE MIDDAY the Alte Post had been taken over by a wedding party. Maggie could hear across the water the sound of their fiddles and guitars, and the blown drifts of singing that grew beerier and gayer as the evening drew in. Several times during the dusk the guests had made brief exploratory sallies down to the water, the women like bright, blown petals swept along in a gale, but each time the showers had driven them in again to their dancing and drinking. The array of lights winked across the lake; the windows had been closed against the rain, and only wisps of music emerged now when some door was opened. Every time that happened, the night seemed to be shaken and convulsed with a distant burst of gigantic laughter.

Maggie went in from the verandah with a few drops of rain sparkling in her hair, and a half-hearted ray of moonlight, the first to break through the clouds, following at her heels. It looked as though they meant to keep up the party all night over there, surely she could have another half-hour of practice before she closed the piano.

The old authentic delight had come back, the intoxication that had been missing for so long. She was alive again, she could sing, she hated to stop singing. When this was over she must get into form quickly, and go back to pick up the wonderful burden. When this was over!

She had not looked ahead at all yet; her vision stopped short, charmed and exalted, at the recognition of her own deliverance. What if that lunch at The Bear had proved only a torment and a frustration? It would not always be so. Francis had promised to come to her here, and he would come; and this time they would be able to talk freely. There had to be respect between them, and an honourable understanding, everything circumstances had made impossible before. It was still true, for all their efforts at noon, that they had never met. Maggie looked forward to their meeting now with passion and impatience; she wanted to know him, and she wanted to be known. The world is too full of impaired and partial contacts that achieve nothing, satisfy no need, do justice to no one. Their relationship should at least close on a better footing than that.

She had the Mahler song settings from "Des Knaben Wunderhorn" on the piano. Contraltos are liable—Tom in one of his sourer moods had once remarked that there was no doubt about it being a liability!—to find themselves expected to include a good deal of Mahler in their recital programmes. Maggie, for her part, had no reservations at all. These full-dress romantic settings of folk-ballads four centuries old might stick in Tom's gullet, but they were strong wine to her.

Ich ging mit Lust durch einem grünen Wald,
Ich hört die Völein singen.

She sang that opening line, and as always it seemed to her a complete song in miniature, with a logical development, a single climax and a perfect resolution.

Many years ago, when she was first learning these songs, she had written in beneath the German words her own attempt at an English singing version. Her unfamiliarity with the original language had worried her, as though it stood between her and the depth of interpretation she wanted. It was easy enough to get someone to provide a literal translation into English, but the meaning divorced from the rhythm and feel of the German had been no help at all. She had wanted a true image, and the only way had been to make one for herself. She never thought of the songs now in her version, she no longer needed these stepping-stones into a world she knew better than her own heart. But in their time they had served their purpose.

> *As forth I went, all in the gay greenwood,*
> *To hear the birds a-singing ...*

She sang it through in the English, with care and wonder, because now it was the English that seemed alien.

Curiously she turned the pages to see what she had made of some of the grander songs. "Wo die schönen Trompeten blasen" belonged to the later set, originally conceived with orchestral accompaniment, and the piano was a poor substitute for those distant, haunting trumpet calls and drum rolls that hung like ominous storm-clouds over the illusion of happy reunion. The soft, brooding introduction came to hesitant life under her fingers, and her voice took up the doubtful, hopeful question with which the song opened:

> *Wer ist denn draussen, und wer klopfet an,*
> *Der mich so leise, so leise wecken kann?*

> *Who's that without there, who knocks at my door,*
> *Imploring so softly, so softly: Sleep no more?*

She had no intention of being asleep when Francis came ...

> *Das ist der Herzallerliebste dein,*
> *Steh' auf und lass mich zu dir ein ...*

> *Your love, your own true love is here,*
> *Rise up and let me in, my dear!*
> *And must I longer wait and mourn?*
> *I see the red of dawn return ...*

... nor of keeping him waiting outside the door, patiently

tapping, like the last time. This meeting had to pay a lot of debts.

> *. . . The red of dawn, two stars so bright.*
> *O that I were with my delight,*
> *With mine own heart's beloved!*

> *The maiden arose and let him in.*
> *Most welcome home, my more than kin,*
> *Most welcome home, my own true love . . .*

She could not help remembering a moment in another hotel room, arms holding her, lips on hers, a voice whispering brokenly: Maggie, forgive me, forgive me! Whether she liked it or not, there was love also to be taken into account. You cannot demand truth, and then select half and throw the inconvenient remainder away. Something would have to be done even about love, if they were to be honest with each other.

> *Ah, do not weep, love, do not pine,*
> *Within the year you shall be mine,*
> *Ere long you shall be one with me*
> *As never bride on earth shall be,*
> *No, none but you on earth, love!*

> *Across the heath to war I fare,*
> *The great green heath so broad and bare . . .*

She sang it through to the end, to the last hair-raising diminuendo among the distant fanfares.

For there, where the splendid trumpets blare and thunder,
There is my house, my house the green turf under.

She would really have to stop this. When the last note of the postlude died away it was so silent that it was borne in upon her guiltily how late it was. Most of the guests must be trying to sleep. Much better, too, if she put out all the lights and seemed to be joining the sleepers; he would find it more difficult to approach if there was light spilling down the staircase into the trees.

She stood for a moment listening, after the lights were out, but everything was quiet and still, not even a thread of song drifted to her across the water. She lay down on the bed in her grey and white housecoat to wait patiently for Francis.

*

She was close to sleep, for all her resolution and eagerness, when the expected tapping came at the glass door on to the verandah. She leaped up gladly, switched on the small bedside lamp, and ran through the sitting-room to whisk aside the curtain and fling the door wide.

The maiden arose, and let him in . . .

The faint light from outside gilded a wet, glistening outline, the shape of a man tall against the sky. The little gleam from the bedroom lit upon the pallid hand that rapped at the glass, and the black stone in the remembered ring on his finger.

The breath congealed in Maggie's throat and the blood in her veins.

This was not Francis, this pale, tense face and shimmering wet body slipping silently into her room, with slow drops coursing down his temples and hair plastered like weed against his forehead. Not Francis, but a drowned man come back out of his grave, out of the lake, out of the past, just when she had allowed herself to be tricked into believing herself rid of him for ever. The rank scent of lake-water and death came over the sill with him, drifting over her in a wave of faintness and nausea. She gave back before him a few steps, and then was stone, unable to move or speak. She was cold, cold, cold as death.

Then everything began to slip away from her, like flesh peeling from her bones, all her delusions of hope, all her belief in the future, any future, even her passion for her own gift. All illusory, all drifting away like dispersed smoke, leaving her naked and lost and damned after all. The world and time came toppling upon her, closing in until there was nothing left but this moment, which was her death.

He came towards her slowly, smiling his pale, drowned smile, his hands held out to her. For what had he come up out of his grave if not to claim her? The hands touched her breast, and cold as she was, she felt their icy chill sear her to the bone. Cold, wet arms went round her and drew her down, down into green depths . . .

Her lips moved, saying: "Robin!" but made no sound. There was a voice whispering in her ear, soft and distant through the darkness that was beginning to wind itself about her:

> *Auf's Jahr sollst du mein Eigen sein,*
> *Mein Eigen sollst du werden gewiss*
> *Wie's Keine sonst auf Erden ist,*
> *O Lieb . . . auf grüner Erden . . .*

Within the year you shall be mine . . . mine as never bride on earth can be . . . No, none on this green earth . . . How could she have disregarded the end? *Mine in my house across the heath, the last dwelling of the drowned . . . the house of green turf . . .*

His face drew near to her, floating through the gathering dark, smiling. When it swam out of focus his lips touched hers, and cold and dark burned into one absolute and overwhelmed her. She sagged in the arms that held her. She experienced death, the death that gave her back to him.

Stooping, the dead man hoisted her slight weight to his shoulder, and carried her away . . .

CHAPTER XI

BUNTY FELSE sat in the gallery at the Alte Post until past eleven o'clock, watching the fun and waiting for George to come home.

For two days, ever since the poacher and the police had fished Friedl Schiffer's body out of the lake, Bunty had been on her own. It was all very well for George to conduct his mild investigations in private, so long as he was merely keeping an eye on two English people apparently involved in something mysterious and possibly dangerous, but not known to be in any way criminal; but murder was quite another matter. So George had gone to the local police with his part of the story, and Bunty had been left to take care of herself from that moment on. What they had made between them out of their pooled information was more than she could guess, but its result had been to provide George with an English-speaking plainclothes-man and a car, with *carte blanche* to shadow Francis Killian's movements as he thought fit. As for the girl, she was safe enough at the Goldener Hirsch; the hotel was under police surveillance, and she had showed no inclination to try to go anywhere, except for a walk into the town to have lunch, surprisingly enough, with her compatriot at The Bear, a meeting which could hardly have been as unplanned as it appeared. And even there they had been directly under George's eye, whether they knew it or not. Bunty hadn't seen him since he walked into the restaurant on Maggie's heels, and left his wife to slip back alone to the Alte Post, before either of those two caught a glimpse of her.

She arrived just in time to relieve the lunch-time loneliness of the elderly Englishwoman who had accidentally got herself included in a predominantly young party, at this tag-end of the holiday season, and found herself ruthlessly shaken from their every activity. To be honest, she was a bore, and Bunty had a certain amount of sympathy with the young people; but since there was no chance of being useful to George for the rest of the day, she resigned herself cheerfully enough to filling a gap for someone else.

The elderly Englishwoman was fascinated and repelled by the wedding party, which was a great deal more rumbustious and well-lubricated than any at which she had ever been a guest. The enormous energy of those young men and their strapping girls seemed to her slightly indecent, and even the lustiness of the music had a strongly earthy flavour about it. The boys might all be in their best dark suits and dazzlingly white shirts, but they still looked as ebulliently fleshy and muscular as in their everyday leathers, and the pointed town shoes pounded the wooden floor as solidly as local hand-made mountain boots. And that awful man who seemed to be cheer-leader and master of ceremonies, the one with the beery paunch and the brick-red face who had always a girl in one hand and a two-litre stein in the other, such a man as that, totally uninhibited, simply could not happen in England. The elderly Englishwoman had, Bunty had discovered, run through two husbands, and one of them had been a butcher and the other a brewer, which made her views rather more surprising. Either the quality of English butchers and brewers was in decline, or she was remembering them rather as she would have had them than as they had been.

The master of ceremonies was, in fact, rather a splendid figure, over six feet high and nearly as wide, with a roaring laugh and the true mountain bass voice, straight out of a square mile of cavern. He was the one who kept leading little forays out into the mild evening, to see if it had yet stopped raining. If it cleared, he would have them all tumbling out to the hotel boat-house, with arms full of food and hands full of bottles, to embark with their musicians and their instruments and their inexhaustible energy on the pewter surface of the Scheidenauersee.

The bride and 'groom had long departed, seen off with the

maximum of noise and every traditional joke. The elderly
Englishwoman said good night and went off to bed, but the
party showed no sign of ending as long as food, drink and
breath held out. Now Helmut was charging out by the
garden door for the fiftieth time, and out there one of the
girls was hallooing that it had stopped raining and the moon
was out. There was loud and hilarious conference, and the
musicians began to pack up their music and stands. Might as
well see the aquacade set off, Bunty thought, and went up
to her room over the lake.

They would be a little time yet, they were hunting for
lanterns to take with them, to turn the night into a carnival.
Bunty took her hair brush to the open window, and looked
at the long, comfortable bulk of the Goldener Hirsch, high
above the trees. Several lights were still burning there, and
several windows uncurtained, so that an ethereal golden haze
brooded over the crest of the hill, as though a swarm of
fireflies had clustered there. As she watched, one or two of
the lights blinked out. Maggie's two windows were already
dark. No, not quite, in the inner one there was a glow-worm
spark that must be the bedside lamp. A convalescent like
Maggie should sleep early and long.

Down beneath Bunty's window three wedding guests, the
vanguard of the flotilla, were opening the boat-house. On
impulse Bunty turned back into the room, and went to look
for George's binoculars. She was not sleepy, and this promised to be quite a night. If only she had happened to catch
Helmut's hospitable eye, down there in the hall, she could
probably have got herself an invitation to join the party;
everyone who was willing was welcome. Free transport
across the lake to that lovely and sinister shore where Friedl
had died, two nights ago. Not that there would be anything
relevant to find there, after the police had combed the whole
stretch of woodland thoroughly. They had found merely
several trampled places, hardly very informative where tourists were accustomed to walk, sit and picnic even thus late in
the year, and one photograph, half-buried in long grass

among the trees. It had not been there longer than a day or two, or the previous rains would have reduced it to a pulp; and the implications were too obvious to resist. Robin Aylwin, George had guessed, on being shown the thing, though he could not positively know whether he was right or not. And at his request they had showed it to Bunty; and Bunty did know. It was a long time ago, but Bunty, after all, had handled not only the bookings but also the publicity on that tour. It was not merely a matter of knowing the faces; she knew the photograph.

The glasses were powerful, and seemed to find light where the naked eye could find none, though she realised as soon as she looked again without them that the moon had emerged again, and was pouring a pale wash of silver across the surface towards the farther shore. Below her several boats were rocking gently on the water, and a shouting, laughing company was piling aboard food, drink, lanterns, guitars, game girls and husky boys. Oars rattled hollowly into rowlocks, there was a good deal of scuffling and scrambling for places. Bunty heard a motor sputtering experimentally; that would surely be Helmut, whose ambition knew no bounds. She lengthened the focus of the glasses again, and made a thoughtful sweep along the shore opposite, just as the wave of moonlight reached it. It looked almost close enough to touch. She fixed on the forward wash of the tide of light, and let her sweep keep pace with it; and for a moment she felt like a surf-rider. Round towards the bowl of darkness below the Goldener Hirsch, stroking the advancing light across the close-set trunks of the trees like fingers over the strings of a harp.

Thus she saw by pure chance, and was the only one to see, the figure that suddenly lunged forward out of the trees beneath the hotel. A man, tall, curiously top-heavy, bursting straight out of the shadow towards the water. The licking tongue of light found pallor about his shoulders, darkness below, a head bent somewhat forward. It had no time to find features or inform her of details, though her eyes in that instant had photographed more than she realised; for at that same moment Helmut got his motor-boat rocketing into life, and with a huge bass-baritone bellow of triumph shot out across the lake, a torch spearing the air before him and a lantern glowing bravely at the stern, three blonde girls trailing scarves in the slip-stream, and the first three or four rowing boats labouring valiantly after.

The figure at the edge of the trees recoiled on the instant, and vanished into cover. Appearing and disappearing were almost one movement, so abruptly was he come and gone. There had been a lift of the head, alert to record the gaily-coloured invasion of his solitude, a glimpse of a regular oval of pallor that told her nothing about his face except that he was clean-shaven. But the vehement movements said young and the aplomb of his responses said he was as quick on the uptake as a wild beast. Bunty ranged the whole rim of the lake there, and tried to penetrate the belt of trees, but she saw no more of him, and no movement to indicate where he passed.

There was, however, nothing about him that could possibly be imaginary, not even in retrospect. Bunty lowered the glasses, and watched the hilarious progress of Helmut's aquacade towards the very curve of shore where the apparition had emerged and vanished. She was unreasonably disturbed. Who recoils like that from being observed by good-natured, harmless souls bent on nothing but fun? Poachers? Where poachers had the sympathy of most people, barring officials, it seemed far-fetched.

True, now she came to think of it, that top-heavy appearance of his, and the slight stoop, the bending of the head, these were all consistent with the fact that he had been carrying something. Something pale. Why else that pallor there at his shoulder? It wasn't warm enough to be running around at night in shirt-sleeves. That was it, he had been hurrying head-forward, bent under something he carried ... And as soon as she had thought of it in those terms, she was almost certain it could not have been a net, even if night-poachers here used a net. No, something heavier than that. Nets are nylon now, they weigh almost nothing. This man had been carrying a considerable weight. Not too much for him, he had moved freely and forcefully under it. Nevertheless, something heavier than a net.

Heavy and pale, and turning him into an asymmetrical shape. The bulk poised on one shoulder.

A small core of ice seemed to spring to life in Bunty's heart. For the more she thought about that shape draped upon the stranger's shoulder, the more did it put on a positive and eloquent form, and confront her, in spite of all her sound, sensible scepticism, with the idea of a girl's limp body in a light-coloured garment, something long and wide-skirted, a housecoat or a negligee. Her weight nicely balanced on the man's shoulder, one arm and hand dangling. Nets don't have hands, whatever they have! Was she imagining it now, after the event?

But why should he start back and hide himself so promptly, so instinctively, if his movements were innocent? And where, come to that, was he heading in such a hurry before Helmut scared him away? For he had started out of the trees at speed, straight towards the water. And there was no boat in all that sweep of shore, no landing stage below the hotel, nothing but the strip of gravel and then dark water.

She reached this point, and the short hairs rose on her neck. What business could he have had with the lake at this hour? What, except the business someone had had with Friedl? Maybe he was still there, somewhere among the trees in hiding, waiting for the revellers to get tired at last, and go home to bed.

And then?

She had a feeling that she was imagining things, probably making the world's fool of herself. But one girl had been drowned, only two nights ago. And that had been murder.

Bunty made up her mind. There was another girl at the heart of this affair, and where could be the harm in making sure that she was safe in her bed? Midnight or not, there was no sense in waiting; and after all, they had known each

other once, however briefly and however long ago. She
dropped George's glasses on the bed, and went straight
downstairs to the telephone booth in the hall.

*

Gisela, startled out of her beauty sleep by the extension
'phone beside her bed, was scandalised at the very suggestion.

"But Miss Tressider went to her room at nine o'clock, she
will have been asleep for a long time. I cannot disturb her.
Can it not wait until to-morrow, if you are staying in Scheidenau?"

"No," said Bunty crisply, "it can't. Or at least, that's
exactly what I want to find out, whether it can or not. I tell
you what, you have keys, you slip up and have a look if she's
all right, and if she is, I'll call her to-morrow."

Though even so, she thought doubtfully, there were other
girls who might equally be in danger, supposing Friedl's
killer was a random defective just breaking out after long
harmlessness. What mattered was whether she had really
seen what she supposed. But always her mind came back to
Maggie. Who else stood so hapless and so alone in the storm-
centre of all these happenings?

"I am sorry," said Gisela indignantly, "I cannot do such a
thing."

"All right, then," said Bunty. "I can! I'm coming over."

*

Gisela was waiting for her in the vast vaulted lobby of
the Goldener Hirsch when she arrived, out of breath, a
quarter of an hour later. It would have been quicker to get
Helmut to ferry her over, but Helmut was weaving inspired
circles round the grouped rowing boats in the centre of the
lake, and his massed choir was singing, pleasantly enough
but very loudly:

> *Heute blau und Morgen blau*
> *Und übermorgen wieder,*
> *Ich bin dein, und du bist mein,*
> *Und froh sind uns're Lieder.*

Gisela, huddled in a red dressing-gown, was by this time rather less indignant and considerably more uneasy. What was the use of pretending no harm could come to anyone in this house, after Friedl?

"I have been up to her room. Everything is in order there, her door is locked and her light out. I am sure she is asleep. I tapped gently, but she didn't answer, and I do not like to disturb her rest."

But her eyes were round and anxious, even afraid. Bunty understood. Somebody had to take the matter farther, now, but Gisela didn't want the responsibility. What Miss Tressider's friend insisted on doing was her own affair.

"The small light in her bedroom is still burning," she said gently. "She has a door on the verandah, hasn't she? Is there a way up from outside?"

"Oh, yes!" Gisela jumped at the idea. "I will show you. We can go through the house." And with luck, if they found the guest in Number One fast asleep, then they could all lock up and go to bed, and no one but themselves would ever be any the wiser about this night alarm.

They passed through the long corridor to the rear of the house, and out by a short passage on to the path from the terrace, and came to the fringe of the trees. A little way along in the darkness was the wooden staircase that led up to the verandah. Bunty felt her way up it by the rough wooden handrail, and half-way up her fingers, sliding along the wood, encountered a jagged knot, and a fragment of something silken soft and fine, like long strands of mohairs, that clung to her skin with the live persistence of synthetic fibres convulsed with static. She pulled the strands loose from the rough place where they had caught, and shut them in her palm as they went on up the stairs.

Gisela hung back, quivering. "The door . . . it is open!"

The glass door stood wide on the darkness of Maggie's sitting-room. Through the half-open door that led to the bedroom beyond, the small gleam of the bedside lamp illuminated for them a pillow still covered by a hand-crocheted bedspread. The pillow was dented by the pressure of a head; so, when they put on the light to look round the room, was the bed itself by a light body. But no one was there now. The verandah door must have been open for some time, for rain had blown in . . . No, that was impossible. The verandah was not completely roofed in, but the jut of the eaves above covered a good half of it, and there had been almost no wind to drive the showers. Yet there was a damp patch just inside the doorway, slightly darkening the scrubbed boards. Everything was tidy, everything was normal, but nothing remained of Maggie Tressider except the score of Mahler's "Wo die schönen Trompeten blasen" on the piano, and in Bunty's palm a small triangle of material woven from one of the more expensive synthetics, printed in a delicate feather pattern of grey and white, like fine lace, with a few long strands of silky nylon fringe trailing from it.

Gisela looked at it and moistened her lips. "It is from the girdle of her housecoat. I have seen her wearing it."

"Yes," said Bunty, "I thought it might be. We've got no choice now. You can see that, can't you? Don't worry, it isn't your fault, I'll do the talking. You go down and call the police. And better tell Herr Waldmeister, he'll have to know. I'll wait here. Tell them the message is from the wife of Detective-Inspector Felse. They'll understand."

*

They understood and they came, with all the more alacrity because they had already received, some ten minutes previously, Werner Frankel's call from a mountain inn over the border in Germany. By the time they reached Bunty, waiting for them in Maggie's sitting-room, there were police patrols out in Germany checking all cars between the border and Felsenbach for a middle-aged light-brown Dodge with a Swiss registration, and Austrian police patrols converging from Langen and Bregenz on Scheidenau, watching for a dark-blue or black Mercedes in a hurry.

It sounded complicated enough without any new complications; but it was becoming quite clear that it was all one case, and too large for taking any chances. First an associate of Miss Tressider was ambushed and abducted on the high-road; and now the girl herself, it seemed, had vanished from her hotel room without warning or explanation.

Not, however, without trace. There were traces enough. A shred torn from her girdle by a knot in the handrail of the staircase. An unimpressive and rapidly drying patch of damp inside her verandah door. And down the slope towards the water, under her windows, search produced a silver chiffon ribbon, still loosely knotted, with one or two dusky gold hairs twined in the knot. It had caught in the fir branches where the half-grown trees grew close, and just at the height of a woman's shoulders. As if she had run from her room, leaving the door open, and straight down the slope in a frenzy of resolution and despair into the lake.

"Yes," said Bunty, bolt upright on the piano stool, "that's what we were meant to think." She stabbed a finger emphatically at the music on the stand. "Even this could be part of the picture. She has a recent history of illness, and has been investigating the disappearance of a man who toured with her here when she was just beginning. That's what it looks like, anyhow. The man in the photograph, yes. And now it seems he's dead. And here is she running through a song like this, all about the demon lover coming back from the grave to claim his bride. If she drowned herself, people might be shocked, but I don't suppose anyone would find it incredible." She added after a moment's thought: "Except, perhaps, this man Killian. He seems to have got nearer to her than anyone."

"And he," said the man in charge dryly, "has been taken care of at the same time, eh?"

She never got the police ranks of Austria clear in her mind, but his name, it seemed, was Oberkofler. He was probably in the sixties, a tall, rangy, mountain man with a wrinkled leather face and shaggy grey hair. He wore whatever had come to hand first when his subordinates got him out of bed, and most of it was non-uniform, but he still had no difficulty in looking like the holder of authority. He was Scheidenau born and bred, and looked the part. Bunty found him impressive. She was glad he was the one among them who spoke English, it gave her an excuse for staying in his vicinity.

"Four of them to take care of the man," he mused, eyeing the damp patch now barely visible on the floorboards, "and one to account for the woman. You are sure he did not come back to the lake later?"

Bunty glanced towards the window. The strains of "Du kannst nicht treu sein" were borne bravely across the water. "How could he?" she said simply.

"Yes . . . I think first we must make contact with our friends there, and make sure that they remain effective, all night if need be. That will make any drowning 'accident' impossible, and any retreat by water, also. From what you tell me it seems that this man must be still somewhere close, perhaps still in the woods. Also, we hope, the lady . . . And now, Frau Felse, if you would wish to get some sleep . . ."

"I'd rather stay," said Bunty. "At least until we get word from my husband." But she meant rather, until we recover those two alive, and find out what this thing is all about. She had begun this hunt, she wanted to see it ended. There were police converging on Scheidenau from all directions, methodically threading the woodland along the lake-shore, a small army mustering because of what George and she had loosed in this quiet village. She intended to see finished what they had begun.

"Then of course you may stay. Where should we have been without you? You can rest here in your friend's room, why not?"

But he showed neither surprise nor disapproval when she followed him down to the office where he had set up his headquarters.

*

The telephone was busy almost every moment for the next

hour, but they found no further trace of Maggie Tressider. The revellers on the lake sang and rowed on unflagging, which in its way was as astonishing as it was admirable. It would have been only human to tire and long for sleep as soon as they were officially requested to go on celebrating. Outside among the trees the search proceeded, inside here Oberkofler directed and co-ordinated. The Waldmeister parents, philosophical and phlegmatic, not to say faced with their usual working day in a few hours' time, accounted for themselves and went back to bed, the sons volunteered their services and went to join in the hunt. And Bunty watched and listened and waited, and harried her memory for any submerged detail or any hopeful idea; and worried now not only about those two hapless people lost, but also about George, from whom there had been no word.

A call from Werner Frankel, over in Felsenbach. The Dodge must have got through before they had an effective block-up. They were getting out a general call on it, and hoped to pick it up somewhere near Regenheim.

Another call from Werner, half an hour later. They had returned now to the scene of the abduction, and found in the ditch where the attack took place a wallet containing the papers of Francis Killian, together with several photographs of a certain gravestone in the cemetery at Felsenbach.

"Of which," said Oberkofler, "perhaps you have heard from the Herr Inspektor?"

"He told me about it yesterday," said Bunty. "The day before yesterday, I mean." She was a little lightheaded with so much waiting and thinking, and so little sleep. "But I haven't seen it. George didn't have a camera. Our mistake!"

And at last, just before one o'clock, another telephone call which Oberkofler answered in voluble German, to switch suddenly and wonderfully into English.

"Yes . . . yes, good, I will send you every man I can, and more as they come in. Yes, your wife is here. Please, only a word . . ." He held out the receiver to Bunty with a smile as wide and deep as the sea. "Your husband, Frau Felse."

"George?" said Bunty, heaving a deep sigh. "Did he tell you? We've lost Maggie as well."

"Yes, I know. That makes us quits, love, I lost the car they had Killian in. Ran head-on into a patrol from Bregenz coming to meet us. We had a mile of road to comb for whatever hole they dived into, but it turned out there's only one, apart from farm-tracks. This one's blind, too, it goes to the lake and stops, so they tell me. Doesn't even pass anything, except that rubble that used to be Scheidenau Castle. But somewhere up there is where they must be. There isn't anywhere else. We're off to hunt for the car now."

"George, isn't there anything I can do to help?"

"From all I hear you've done it," said George. "They also serve . . . ! If we find him, the odds are we find her, too. This is all one set-up. Keep hoping! Sorry, got to clear this line, it may be wanted."

"Yes, of course. See you, then!"

She held out the receiver to Oberkofler, but he shook his head at her and smiled. She hung up. She was suddenly shaking with reaction, and dared not try to guess how the night would end.

Distantly, inexhaustibly, across the lake and in at the window came the thunder of the guns of Helmut's navy:

> *Es war einmal ein treuer Hussar,*
> *Der liebt sein Mädchen ein ganzes Jahr,*
> *Ein ganzes Jahr, und noch viel mehr . . .*

CHAPTER XII

TWO VOICES were discussing her above her head. They didn't know that dead people can hear. Quite dispassionate voices, cool, leisurely and low, discussing her in terms of life and death. Either they had no bodies, or dead people can't see. She was dangling just below the level of consciousness, clinging to the surface tension like the air-breathing nymph of some water creature.

"*So schön auch,*" said the first voice critically.

"Nobody's beautiful who gets in my way," said the second voice in plain English and without overtones; a light, pleasant, untroubled tenor voice without a care in the world.

"*Aber schön,*" the first voice insisted with detached approval. "She has everything!"

"Except immortality."

"What are you going to do with her?"

The second voice was silent long enough to indicate a shrug of the shoulders. "Did I make her wade in here so far out of her depth? She had a death wish."

"Waste of a girl!" said the first voice with impersonal regret.

"There are others. Even some with perfect pitch." And in a blithe half-tone the second voice began to sing to itself dreamily:

> *Mein Eigen sollst du werden gewiss,*
> *Wie's Keine sonst auf Erden ist,*
> *O Lieb . . . auf grüner Erden . . .*

Any moment now she would feel the prick of the needle in her thigh, and submerge again. So this must be hell. What could be more absolute hell than to have to go on living and reliving these few weeks to eternity, trying to escape from the net, believing she had escaped, only to find herself back at the beginning and trapped as fast as ever? Everything to do again, everything to suffer again, everything to lose again. No, not quite a duplication, this time the dialogue had changed. The decision last time had been for life. This time it was for death.

Then, in the moment that she broke surface and knew herself conscious, miraculously the burden was gone. Last time she had awakened alone, oppressed and appalled by the horror of guilt without a source. Now that the verdict was for death she awoke to the calm and lightness of deliverance. She had not been deceived, after all, her guilt had been only a delusion, a sickness of which she was healed at last. Even if she died now, it would be as a whole, a sane person.

For this second voice she knew very well, and it belonged firmly in this world and no other. It was no poor injured ghost that had come to fetch her away, but a living and dangerous man, and he had come not because she owed him a death, but because she was a threat to him alive. Her probing had begun to uncover him of the carefully cultivated invisibility of years, he could not afford to let her go on with it. Grave or no grave, memorial or no memorial, Robert Aylwin was alive. She had neither killed him nor done him any wrong; and even if he killed her, she would never again be truly in his power, never his victim as she had been all these years. Neither living nor dead would Robin ever stand between her and love again.

*

She opened her eyes upon low stone vaulting that had a worn and monumental grandeur, like a feudal hall before luxury came into fashion. She was lying on a rough grey blanket spread upon a stone settle built all along one wall, and in the wall itself she saw the round fretted grooves left by the ends of barrels. The flagged floor was sifted with fine sand, the accumulated dust of wind erosion and time. The air felt moist and cool. There was a dim light from one heavily shaded electric bulb, that showed her only the side of the room where she lay, and a glimpse of a door in the corner, a door not worn at all, but surely almost new and very solid.

"*Achtung!*" said the first voice very softly. "She's coming round. Shall I . . .?"

"No, let her! Company will help to pass the time until those fools go home to bed."

She could see the pair of them only up to the shoulders, for the dark shade over the light obscured their faces. One of them stepped back accommodatingly into the shadows, the other came forward and sat down on one hip on the edge of the settle beside her feet. He saw that her eyes were wide-open and fixed upon his face, and turned the lamp deliberately to let it illuminte him fully.

"Allow me! Is that better?"

He no longer glistened and streamed, the fall of wavy hair was nearly dry, only the unruly way it curled round his forehead showed that he had recently been out in the rain. He must have stood outside her room under the dripping trees all the while she was singing, waiting for the appropriate moment. He must, she thought, have been amused by the Mahler; a little Gothic horror would appeal to his sense of humour. He was dressed to go invisibly in the dark, in clerical grey slacks and a thick black sweater with a polo neck; the same, perhaps, in which he had prowled the woods that night he throttled and drowned Friedl.

Looking at him now, she found nothing surprising in that. He sat smiling at her, a cigarette held delicately between forefinger and thumb, narrowing his eyes slightly against the smoke that drifted towards his face in a light draught. The same boyish, regular features, the same full, mobile, strongly curling lips for ever on the edge of laughter. He laughed a great deal, always, at everything. For years she had forgotten the colour of his eyes, lowered in Friedl's photograph, closed in that dead faun's face over his grave. Perhaps it had cost her an extra effort to forget them, and she had managed it only because it was essential. They watched her now steadily, curiously, pale greenish-gold eyes, round and bold, a goat's eyes, intelligent, inscrutable, malicious. The eyes laughed, too, almost without cease, but at some private joke that was not for ordinary humans. He was hardly older than he had been thirteen years ago, when she had last seen him. Why should he be, when he lived—it was to be seen in the debonair face and the cool, bright eyes—immune from all feeling and all responsibility?

She drew herself up with an effort to sit upright, her back —how appropriately!—against the wall. Never for a moment did her eyes leave his face.

"It *is* you," she said at last, "it was *you* behind everything!" She braced her hands against the cold stone to take fast hold of reality. She knew her situation now, and her enemy. She had marvellously recovered the fullness of life only just in time to lose it again, and feel the loss double. But also she had now a double stake for which to put up a fight. "So you *are* alive," she said.

"Dear Maggie," he said, lazily smiling, "I believe so."

"Then what *was* it I heard, that night? *What was it that went into the lake?*"

She thought for a moment that he was not going to answer her, but with a captive audience, and all the cards and all the strings in his own hands, and time to kill—*but how did it happen that he had time to kill?*—why not talk? After all, she wasn't going anywhere, was she, to repeat anything he might let fall? He could indulge his fancy with no risk to himself.

"Just one of old Waldmeister's stacked logs," he said serenely. "The whole clearing down by the water was full of them, he surely couldn't grudge me one in a good cause."

"But *why*?" she said almost inaudibly, wrenching at the wanton shaft that had broken off short in her spirit as in wounded flesh, and festered ever afterwards. "Why play me such a trick? Why did you have to *die* at all? And even if you had your reasons for wanting to vanish, why stage a scene like that with me first? Why pretend you loved me? Why ask me . . ." She drew breath slowly, and flattened her shoulders warily against the wall; the chill pierced her like a gust of cold air, and every such minute shock of reality helped to calm her senses and clear her mind. She, too, could talk; words were there to be used for her purposes as well as his. The more attention he gave to her, to impressing and subduing her, even to amusing himself with her, the less he would have left for imagining any counter-attack. "Just think," she said, eyeing him narrowly from under the fall of her loosened hair, "I might even have accepted you! What would you have done then?"

He found the recollection of that night rather flattering, she thought; maybe his memory even embroidered it. But be careful of believing that. Conceit is only a discardable toy to a man without feelings.

"I should have married you, of course," he said sunnily. "It wouldn't have been too great a hardship. You'd have turned out quite a profitable investment, the way things have gone. And as my wife, you wouldn't have been asked to give evidence against me, either—would you?"

So that was one more piece of the puzzle falling into place. He had flicked it into her lap deliberately, she knew that. Nevertheless, record it, Maggie! He's quite sure of his security, but there are things even he doesn't know. He may yet live to regret dropping these small golden apples to distract you into running about at his will.

"I see," she said thoughtfully. "But what was I supposed to be able to tell? I never knew there *was* anything to be told against you."

He leaned back to prop himself against the wall by one wide, lean shoulder, and grinned at her amiably through the smoke of his cigarette.

"Do you remember the spring trip we made that year with the Circus?"

"Well, well!" she said. "You've still got the terms pat, after all this time."

"Dear Maggie, I have as near as damn it total recall. I remember the whole ramshackle set-up, and you so dedicated and earnest, and such an easy touch. You remember carrying some expensive cosmetics through Customs for me, that spring? A girl could get by with declaring those jars, when a man would automatically get charged on them. And it turned out that way, didn't it? And a friend of mine met us at the boat-train, and I handed the whole works over as a present for his sister. Dear Maggie, you can't have forgotten that kind deed? After all, what did you ever have to declare, except sheet music and gramophone records?"

What money had she ever had, in those days, to buy any

but the most vital necessities, all of which were comprehended in music? But all she said was: "I remember."

"Well, they picked up my anonymous friend later that year with rather a lot of heroin on him. Yes, that's what was in the jars, sealed below about an eighth of an inch of cream and stuff. We were in Basel on the autumn tour when I got word, so I had to make up my mind quickly what to do. There was no knowing for sure that he'd keep his mouth shut about me, and even if he did, there might still be something they could hook up to me. And if ever they had found their way to the Circus, you'd soon have told them how those cosmetics came into England, wouldn't you? It all boiled down to a choice between marrying you to close your mouth, and going home and chancing my luck, or staying here and turning professional. They'd been inviting me to do that for a year or more."

"*They?*" said Maggie gently.

"What good would it do you if I named names, my dear? The whole set-up has changed since then. Just one organisation among many, until I made it over to my taste. Call it what you like. *Cosa mia* . . ."

Yes, clearly anything into which he entered would soon have to become "*his thing*"; he wasn't interested in being a subordinate. Perhaps that was why he'd never bothered to work at music, because even the disciplined approach necessary was only going to get him into the third, or at best the second, rank. "So you'd been smuggling for them for some time," she said, "under cover of Freddy's respected name."

"Every trip. You'd helped me once before. Oh, not always hard drugs, in fact, very seldom. Anything light and profitable, precious stones, lenses, passports, medicines, even watches when other fields were dull. Once I went into England with two medieval manuscripts among my sheet music. We had a customer waiting for those, of course. Miniatures, rare coins, stamps, small art items—anything portable enough and expensive enough. We provide a worldwide service, moving the goods to where the demand is.

Even before the crunch came I'd been thinking of throwing up the Circus before it threw me up, and going into the business full-time. It looked as if my career with Freddy was nearly up in any case. I let *you* make up my mind for me. *You* turned me down, *they* got me. You even provided me with a reason for suicide, if people got too nosy, though I admit the log was an afterthought. I remember taking off down the hillside, and there were these stacks of wood ready for carting, and it was too good to miss. You were so damned confident and secure, it seemed an appropriate gesture to give you something else to think about besides your great future."

"It must have been a disappointment to you," she said dryly, "when I didn't tell anybody the story you'd so thoughtfully set up for me to tell."

He leaned his head back against the wall and laughed aloud.

"I was shocked to find you capable of such duplicity. You didn't want any scandals or other little stumbling-blocks in the way of your career, did you? But after all, it worked out very well. Friedl kept me informed. If everyone had accepted Freddy's dark hints, and come to the conclusion that I'd simply run out to avoid minor unpleasantness, that was fine with me. Just so long as nobody started a serious search for me *alive*."

"Friedl was your creature? One of the organisation?"

"Hardly that. Let's say Friedl became a useful camp follower. One of our ears on the world. One of our tongues, too, though," he added candidly, "I ought to have known better."

"Then it was you who put her up to telling all those lies to Francis and to me, to prove that you were dead?"

"To Killian, yes. But to you? There she exceeded her orders, she had her own bone to pick with you. Friedl . . ." He hoisted one shoulder in a smooth and eloquent gesture. "She always preferred to lie rather than tell truth, if not for policy, then for pleasure. Her facility has been useful on occasions, but when she was mad with jealousy—oh, yes, hadn't you realised that?—she was a menace. She talked altogether too much. When she put you on to the grave, that was the end. She had to go. Probably the grave was a mistake from the beginning, I should have let well alone. But at the time it seemed a heaven-sent opportunity to have a second line of defence ready, in case of need. And then *you* had to get too interested in it, of all people, and of all people *you* would never have swallowed it. Anybody else she might have told, but *you* . . ."

"I've seen the photographs," said Maggie. "How did you even manage that affair? Was it you who provided the body? *Is* there really a body there?"

"Oh, yes, there's a body, just as she told you. He came down with the snow water in the thaw. No, that wasn't any master-stroke of mine, he was pure luck. I don't suppose anyone will ever know who he really was. No, all I did was take the chance when it offered. Then there'd always be a grave to which I could misdirect enquiries if ever I needed to suggest my own death. It was a body, male, near enough my height and build and age, and past being identified. All I needed to do was make the anonymous offer to pay for his burial, as an act of piety, and make sure the death of an unknown young man was recorded and dated. Nothing so crude as a false identification or a name, of course. The portrait was an afterthought, a *jeu d'esprit*. Maybe too impudent, but it amused me."

"So you have a monumental mason in your pocket, too," said Maggie admiringly.

"We have one of everything we need," he agreed calmly.

"You must have risen rapidly in the organisation."

"To the top. Some years ago now. Class tells," he said demurely, and his lips curled in the very same private laughter he had allowed the mason to engrave on the tombstone, giving the lie to the depersonalised brow and marble eyelids, turning the dead mask into a living demon.

"And then," he said reproachfully, "*you* had to come along and start looking for me—you, who weren't going to swallow that grave without gagging. If you hadn't turned so curious, after all this time, none of this need have happened. For God's sake, *why did you?*"

She stared back at him wordlessly for a long minute, herself marvelling to find the landscape of her mind so miraculously changed. "I had you on my conscience," she said with deliberation. "I believed I owed you a life."

Very softly, and with the most beguiling of smiles, he agreed: "*And so you do.*"

It could hardly be a surprise. She had known all along that she had gone too far to be left alive. Would he be talking to her like this, otherwise? From the beginning she had known at the back of her mind that she was talking chiefly to engage his attention, to make him forget time, to gain minutes as best she could. Because of the one thing he did not know about that Mahler performance of hers tonight, the fact that she had been waiting for the arrival of another visitor.

What if Francis was late in coming? He would come. And whatever others might think at finding her bedroom empty —that she had gone off of her own will, to some appointment in the woods, to somebody else's bed, to the bottom of the lake—Francis would know better. Francis would know that she had been waiting for him, and that nothing would have induced her to leave the appointed place until he came. And whether he called in the police or not, he would begin a search for her on his own account until he found her.

On that one chance she pinned her hope, and saw that it was still a substantial hope. No point in over-estimating it, though. For Robin wouldn't be killing time with her in this idle way, however enjoyably, if he himself were not waiting for something.

At least go on talking, she thought. At least keep him from deciding not to wait, after all.

"How do you intend to dispose of me?" she asked conversationally.

His bright, probing, inscrutable yellow stare was fixed and blinding upon her face, and for once he was not smiling.

"My dear girl, you set the whole scene yourself. Here are you with a recent record of illness and odd behaviour, and apparently with some sort of obsession about me, a small, sad episode in your distant past. And then your rest-home is invaded by a tragedy—a girl drowned in the lake. Suiside is infectious. Now they're going to find your verandah door open, and a nice little trail laid down to the shore. I've seen to that. And on your piano, just as you left it, that wonderfully appropriate Mahler song about the dead lover returning by night to visit his beloved ... Oh, yes, someone will be able to make the connection. With that sort of background, who's going to be surprised that you finally ran off the rails altogether, and did away with yourself?"

"Then why didn't you slip me into the water right away, while you had the chance?"

He laughed gaily. "Because there's a plague of drunken wedding guests holding a regatta all round the lake. And a damned inconvenient moment they chose to embark."

"That's a matter of opinion," said Maggie tartly.

"Granted. But they'll get sick of it just now, and go home to bed. Don't worry, to-morrow the police will be dragging for your body."

"And of course," she said, "they'll find it?"

"Oh, yes, they'll find it. Quite definitely death by drowning, there'll be no injuries to spoil the picture, not even a bruise. A pity I let Friedl make me angry, but what can you do? No, my dear, for a Maggie Tressider they might go on searching too long and too well, if I didn't make them a present of you. They might find other things, one never knows. No, they shall have you gratis."

To make a suicide like that convincing, she reasoned with furious coldness, and to ensure that she was found with satisfying promptness, she would have to be put into the water near to the hotel. So they must be somewhere quite close now. Why not go on doing the direct thing, and ask? He had answered some curious questions already, being quite certain of his security here. But if this waiting continued long enough, and every moment counted, what she had gleaned from him might come in useful yet to convict him.

"Where have you brought me?" She looked round the dim room as though she had just discovered it. There was a second door in the distant wall, directly opposite the first one, as though this was only one in a series of rooms. Cellars? Not in the hotel, surely? Yet he could not have brought her far. The other man sat silent on the far side of the single lamp, decapitated by the sharp edge of the black shade, unconcernedly breaking, cleaning and loading a gun, a pair of large, dexterous hands with no head to direct them, but remarkably agile and competent on their own.

"We're in the wine-cellars of the old castle. There was a whole labyrinth of them originally, but most are blocked up with rubble. We sealed off the safest part of the network as a repository. One of several. With three frontiers so close, we need a safe place handy in each country, where men and things can be got out of sight quickly until the heat is off. No," he said grinning, "don't look round for treasure, we've cleared everything out. After to-night we shan't be using this place again, it's likely to be a little too precarious for our purposes."

"And you, where do you pass the—shall we say 'un-buried'?—part of your life? I suppose you've still got an identity somewhere among the living?"

"Oh, several," he assured her merrily. "Most respectable ones, and in more than one country. As one frontier closes, another opens. To a new man, of course. You know, Maggie . . ." She waited, watching him steadily. He was eyeing her with calculating thoughtfulness, like a sharp trader contemplating an inspired deal. "In a way, it's a pity I couldn't have both, you *and* this. Who'd have thought you'd stay in mourning for me all this time?"

She remembered the anguish he had cost her, the obsessive hold he had had upon her, and suddenly it dawned upon her that Francis had made the same mistake about her that this man was making now. Because she had all but wrecked her life on him, they believed she must have loved him, if only in retrospect after he was gone. She opened her eyes wide, and laughed in Robin's face. It was perhaps the only luxury she had left, and not one that did her any credit, but she could not resist it.

"*In mourning* for you? Do you know what you've been to me? A nightmare, a curse, and that's all . . ."

The man with the gun said: "*Achtung!*" sharply and clearly, and came to his feet.

Maggie's laughter broke off in her throat. She crouched against the wall with head reared, ears straining after those small, stony sounds approaching somewhere outside the door. Robin watched the little sparks of hope come to life softly in her eyes, and the smile shattered by her laughter came back to his lips like a reflection in a pool reshaping itself after the dropping of a stone. He slid from the settle and stretched himself contentedly.

"Too bad, my dear, it isn't what you think."

She had already grasped that it could not be. This was someone who knew the way in here, and approached quietly but without stealth. Not what she had been hoping for; merely what Robin had been waiting for.

The man with the gun crossed to the door and drew back the bolts. Maggie lowered her feet quickly over the edge of the stone shelf and stood up, drawing the folds of her soiled housecoat about her, for it seemed that time had run out.

Into the room walked four men, bringing in with them gusts of the chill night air and the green smell of the wet woods. Two of them were big, raw-boned mountaineers, from which side of the border there was no knowing. The third was slim and lightweight and young, and belted into a wasp-waisted raincoat. The fourth, who was thrust in limping heavily, with blood on his face and a gun in his back, was Francis.

*

Maggie made not a sound, but as if she had cried out to him his gaze flew to her, and fastened on her with such dismay and despair that her heart turned in her; and what

he saw in her face was the mirror image of his own anguish.
The only grain of consolation he had had left was that she
was safe in her bed; the only hope she had been able to
keep was that he would launch the hunt for her in time. Both
bubbles burst and vanished.

Maggie hardly noticed the dwindling of her own small
chance of life in the sudden rush of rage and pain she felt
for him. She had bought this fairly, but what had he done?
She had brought him into this, unarmed and alone against
a highly-organised and ruthless gang, and it was because of
her actions that they were both going to die. She was to
drown, because they wanted her found and accounted for.
But Francis . . . No, better for them if he vanished altogether. What was the good of shutting her eyes? Since they
had taken him prisoner somewhere on the road, perhaps
well away from Scheidenau, why bring him back to this
place if he was ever to leave it again?

Robin and his men were speaking rapid and colloquial
German, Robin questioning, the others answering. She was
soon lost in the language, but the implications were clear
enough. Any trouble? No, no trouble, everything in hand,
everything to numbers. There was something about a car—
Francis's car?—that should be in Klostermann's yard by
now. They were all easy and content, not elated but extract-
ing a certain workmanlike satisfaction out of their efficiency.
Maggie stood almost forgotten, trying to understand,
straining her senses in case there should be something, anything, at which hope could claw as it went by, and find a
hold. For one of them, at least. For Francis! But she knew
there would be nothing now. Just a few hours of deferment,
and they had lost their chance for ever.

His captors had loosed their hold of him as soon as they
had him inside, and the door firmly locked and bolted. Why
not? He was battered and unarmed, and they had several
guns between them. Even Robin had a gun in his hand now,
a tiny, snub-nosed black thing that he dangled on his forefinger like a toy.

Something had been said about her, a question in the

other direction. All three of Robin's men were eyeing her with some concern; no doubt they had expected her to be in the lake by this time.

"Oh, Maggie!" said Robin carelessly, giving her a light glance over his shoulder. "There was a slight hitch there." He had slipped back into English, she thought, not by chance, but so that she should understand. "We shall have to keep her now until the Volga boatmen go home to sleep it off. They're sure to tire sooner or later. Roker's keeping an eye on them upstairs, he'll give us the tip when they quit." He looked back at Francis, and spun the little gun in his hand, and the butt nestled into his palm like a bird homing. "But we may as well get this one underground," he said.

Francis had taken out a handkerchief, and was quietly wiping the blood from his cheek. His face, grey and drawn, kept a total, contained silence. Even when he raised his eyes for an instant to take one more look at Maggie, they gave nothing away beyond a kind of distant, regretful salutation. In the presence of these people he had nothing to say to her, not even with his eyes. The burden of longing and self-blame and love was not something he wanted to display for them or pile upon her at this last moment. As long as he had a card to play—and he had one, the last—he might as well play it, and speak to the point. The rest could stay unsaid; she wouldn't be any the poorer or more unfortunate for ending her life without any declaration from Francis Killian.

"There's one thing you don't know . . . Aylwin," he said, his voice emerging hoarse and clumsy from a bruised throat. "I take it you *are* Aylwin? Who else? Your boys don't know it, either, but all the way up that mountain section there was a car following me to-night. It was on my trail yesterday, too, I couldn't be sure of it then, but I know it now. I thought it was your pack on my heels, till I hit your ambush ahead. There's only one other thing it could be, you know that, don't you? A police car keeping an eye on me. They weren't far behind when this bunch flagged me down. You think they're blind and deaf? Or do you suppose they'd drop their assignment just when it got interesting? They'll be hard after us right now, and there'll be reinforcements on the way. Do you think you're ever going to get out of here unobserved?"

"I think," said Robin, smiling at him lazily, eyes narrowed and golden, "that you are a gallant but hopeless liar, trying the only bluff you've got left. But just to be obliging . . ." He turned to the three who stood watching and listening, and snapped back briskly into German. They shook their heads in vigorous rebuttal, laughing the story away with absolute confidence. "You see? No shadow, no police, no fairy tales. If you had a tail, it got lopped off *en route*. But I think you never had one."

"Your trouble," said Francis levelly, "is that you have to have too much faith in your understrappers. The usual trouble with businesses that get too big. That Dodge will never get as far as Klostermann's. If they miss it in Felsenbach, they'll pick it up before it reaches Regenheim. And in case there's any doubt about the place where I was waylaid, and about *your* tie-in with the affair, let me tell you I've left them my wallet and papers there on the spot. With the whole set of photographs of *your* grave."

The first faint shadow of doubt touched but could not deface Robin's smiling certainty. He turned his head again to shoot orders at his underlings; and they laid hands ungently on Francis and began to turn out his pockets, though they still poured voluble scorn on his story. He raised his hands out of their way, flinching as they handled him.

"No wallet, no passport, no driving licence. You think I came out without those, Aylwin? Don't bother to send a man back to pick them out of the ditch, the police did that long ago. And did you know that there's an English detective in Scheidenau, co-operating with the locals? He followed me from England. Maybe he's the one who's been on my trail all day. He certainly was when we had lunch at The Bear."

"All right, so you left your wallet in the ditch. What good

is it going to do you? Someone will spend your money and throw the rest away. I'll believe in your English detective when I see him. And as for your police tail, Max with your hired job would have run head-on into it round the bend, and got word to me long ago."

"Maybe he did run into it, and they picked him up on the spot. Ever think of that? Better not write them off so easily, Aylwin, they were there, all right." It was his only anchor now, a frail one, but not an illusion. They had been there. God knew what had become of them now, but they might yet find their way where they were needed. "You haven't a hope of getting out of here unseen. Why add more murders to the score? It's long enough already. You might get away with Friedl. Touch Maggie Tressider, and they'll hunt you to the end of the world."

It was breath wasted. Even if he had been subject to intimidation, even if he had believed, Aylwin had gone too far now to turn back. He yawned elaborately in Francis's face, and smiled, reaching up one hand to turn the shade of the lamp, and direct the light towards the darkest corner of the cellar. The circle of pallor flowed across the flagstones like a silent tide. Against the wall a heap of dark earth reared into view, and the rims of two of the stones showed black and thin as pen-strokes.

"Get them up!"

They had crowbars and spades propped in the corner. The slanting light cast monstrous shadows from the stooped shoulders and heads of the two mountain men, as they leaned their weight almost languidly on the crowbars, and the thin black line at one end of the nearer stone broadened into a gash, a gaping rectangle of darkness.

For me, thought Francis, not for Maggie; he said they'd have to keep her until the Volga boatmen went home . . . Boatmen! Yes . . . so someone's balking them from going near the lake. *At this hour?* A grain of hope clung obstinately to life within him, for the police might justify him yet, and come in time for Maggie, though not for him. Bargaining was out of the question, what had he to bargain with?

Certainly not his own life, that was already forfeit. No means even of buying time. If he set out to sell his life as high as he could, there would be bullets flying here, and Aylwin might opt to cut his losses and change his plans, and hurry both his prisoners out of the world and into the ground together. No, nothing left to do but count on the Volga boatmen—whoever they were, thank God for them!—and submit without provocation, and pray that they might be police patrols who would never go home until she was found alive.

Robin Aylwin swung one long leg negligently from the edge of the settle, played with his little pistol, and watched his men at work. A job like any other. He paid no more attention to Francis, and Francis, arrived at the bleak conclusion that there was nothing he could do for Maggie but die submissively, had fallen mute. It was Maggie who broke the silence.

"Francis!"

Never in his life had he heard his name spoken like that. A small, fine-spun, golden, intimate sound, like the marvellous *mezza voce* she could float clean to the back row of the remotest gallery of any opera house in the world, to pierce the last listener's heart as if no one existed but himself and the singer. Out of the centre of one being, and aimed with certainty to reach the centre of another. For no one was present here now but Francis and Maggie. She had excised the others from her own consciousness and she banished them from his. There was only one thing left that she could do for Francis, and she was doing it as well as she knew how.

"Francis, I'm sorry I ever got you into this. Forgive me! But I want to tell you that for my part I'm glad to have known you, even on these conditions. Thank you for everything you've done for me. I don't have to say good-bye. I shan't be long after you."

Robin had turned his head to stare at her. The men leaning hard over the half-open grave froze, and hung watching and listening. And then Robin's head went back with a toss like an angry horse balking, and he uttered a shout of brief and violent laughter. Something in the sound sent his men scurrying back to work on the second stone in haste. Never had Maggie looked at *him* like that, never spoken his name with that particular awareness that suddenly bestowed a greatly enlarged identity. Never had she turned on him this starry face, with blazing, recognising eyes wide-open to love. He had gone to the trouble to stage a beautiful declaration of love for her once, and she had not even heard him. A phoney love, of course! Still, by all the rules she ought to have succumbed.

The flagstones were propped back gently against the wall, uncovering the greyish, hard-packed earth, and the long, narrow hole from which the heap of soil had been dug out already in preparation for a new incumbent. Harsh darkness and a sinister bony light, distorted figures stooped over an open grave. Maggie's mind drifted, recoiling from a present that was unbearable and a future that was non-existent. This was the dungeon scene from *Fidelio*. But Leonora had at least had a pistol, and here all the pistols were on the other side. She had nothing to fight with, nothing with which to defend her own or attack her enemy. "*Ich bin sein Weib!*" No, this would be a *Fidelio* without any ecstatic love duet, without any final triumph for justice . . .

Robin slid from the settle and spread his feet firmly. She saw his thumb slide back the safety catch of the gun. He had forgotten her again; his attention was fixed on the open grave. Business as usual, he had his own affairs to look after, and no emotion had any part in them, not even offended vanity

"You won't be lonely," he said pleasantly, his amber eyes measuring Francis, "you'll be joining the sitting tenant. A fellow-countryman of yours who also got too nosy. The errand-boy always thinks he can run the business better than the managing director."

He raised his hand without haste, and levelled the gun. The grave-diggers and their colleagues drew off from

Francis and stood clear, waiting phlegmatically to fill in the hole again and replace the stones. The long finger on the trigger contracted gently.

Maggie awoke before it tightened to the firing-point. Nothing to fight with? But she *had*! She had one weapon, the ultimate weapon, not effective to stand off death, but a grenade exploding in Robin Aylwin's orderly plans. She had a body he needed unmarked for his own purposes, with lungs that could still breathe in lake-water. She gathered it in a convulsion of vengeful energy, and flung it between Francis and the gun.

CHAPTER XIII

THE GUN WENT OFF, a sharp, spiteful waspish sound, lost in Robin's startled cry. Maggie hung poised in front of Francis with spread arms, and felt him lurch and recover at her back, fending himself off from the wall. There was no pain, no impact, nothing. She had under-estimated the jungle speed of Robin's reactions. In the instant that she moved he had divined her purpose, and methodical in everything he did, had adhered stubbornly to his own intent. The bullet must have been in motion when he flung up his wrist to let it whine in ricochet from the vault above, and bury itself in the wall. He could not avoid her without avoiding Francis, too. Frantically she reached back a hand to feel for Francis, to assure herself that he was there intact, if only for one instant of communion, and to fasten herself to him indivisibly so that he could not be killed without killing her. His arm groped its way about her waist and lifted her. She felt the hardness of his body, and heard him breathing in heavy, painful groans.

But all she saw was Robin's face, and that she would never forget, however long she had for remembering. In the very moment that he had deflected his shot, to keep his prize suicide presentable for an autopsy surgeon and an inquest jury, everything in him had suddenly curdled and changed. Intelligence he had, it worked at the speed of light. The whine of the ricochet was still flittering about the vault like a disturbed bat when the true horror hit him, the thing that undid him utterly. He saw in a blinding vision the full significance of what she had done, and for once in a cold life he reacted without calculation, in a frenzy of irrational jealousy. He had never cared a damn for her, nor did he now, nor would he ever, for her or any woman. And yet it was an intolerable outrage to him that she, who felt nothing for him, should toss her life away willingly for another man. How could it matter to him? He had lived very successfully without need or respect or regard for love, and yet all that impressive erection suddenly crumbled to a mouthful of bitter ashes. It mattered, all right! It mattered to the heart, to the bone, to the marrow of the bone. She had tricked him, cheated him out of his whole achievement. She had done what no one else had ever done, made him feel.

He uttered a shriek of grief and rage, incredible from that composed and imperturbable throat of his, and the comely mask before her broke and crumpled horribly into ugliness. Two round, glaring, golden eyes in a grimacing chaos of hate levelled upon their target for once not coldly but in boiling fury. The bomb that had shattered him had shattered his plans with him. The only thing that mattered now was to kill Maggie Tressider. The little black pistol came up fast and accurately. He fired pointblank at her.

She had clamped her arm over the arm Francis had thrown round her, her hand gripping his hand, he could not throw her clear, she would not let go of him. All he could do was hold her fast and turn with her in his arms, putting her between him and the wall.

The bullet took him in the back of the left shoulder, a little high for where Maggie's heart should have been. The impact drove them both forward against the wall. They slid down it, still linked, still clasping each other, and on the chill, soiled flagstones Maggie drew herself clear, half-stunned by the fall and his weight upon her, and gathered him jealously into her arms. The heat of his blood jetted into the folds of her sleeve. His head lay in the crook of her elbow, his face half-smiling up at her for one astonished instant, before all its precision of line dissolved into faintness, into a dream.

There were no more shots, and yet the vault above them was suddenly alive with discordant noises, none of them understood, none of them relevant. Francis and Maggie were alone in the centre of a whirlwind, in a cone of calm that was half shock and half the peace beyond exhaustion. For a moment she did not even realise that he was hit, she only held him like a trophy, like the palm after a long, hard race.

Then her senses cleared a little, enough to distinguish the hammering at the door, hysterical with alarm, and the clash of the bolts as the man in the raincoat opened. The man who burst in and slammed the door at his back she saw clearly. She saw him clawing at the bolts, turning the key again. Robin had called him Roker, and he spoke English, most likely he *was* English. Why not? They flourish everywhere. If ever they wanted a description of this one, she could give it, one that would find him wherever he ran. Her vision seemed to be inordinately clear, as in one kind of dream. He was a little, fast-moving, quiet man, who even screamed in a whisper; balding, nondescript, fortyish, tough as nylon rope and almost as synthetic, a product of his age. He was rattling out destructive sentences in a low, venomous monotone; and because of him, she and the man she held in her arms were forgotten.

"Police . . . hordes, I tell you! You knew I had the trap open, God damn it, I *had* to! Any minute I might have had to drop in here fast. It wasn't the shot so much . . . somebody screamed like a blasted woman. How could I know they were that close? Don't *ask* me what brought them snooping round here . . . They *are* here! They homed on that squeal like on a radar fix. Don't hope for it, they saw me drop, all right, they know where the stone is. Nothing's going to keep them out of here now. *Sure* I locked and bolted the door up there. You think two doors will hold them long?"

Robin's voice, riding high and authoritative above this hail of disaster, said clearly: "Out, the back way!" All his disintegrated atoms had welded again into one efficient being at the first pressure from outside. He dropped his victims without hesitation, without another thought. If he stayed to silence them he would lose precious time, and leave the police two identifiable bodies and two all-too-provable murders, should he ever be taken to answer for them. If the police here were on to him, then the game in these parts was up for good. Take the gains, cut the losses, and get out clean. There were other continents besides Europe, and there was money already carefully distributed there.

"They must have found the car in the coppice, they came up from that way . . . No, I tell you there wasn't a sign . . . not until that fool yelled like a banshee. Who the hell *was* it? You *knew* I should leave the trap open! They came from everywhere, like greyhounds on a hare . . ."

"All right, we've got the message. Open that door and get going. Scatter and make for Dornbirn."

A crisp, cool, commanding voice, not at all the scream of a banshee now. And they were obeying him in something more than haste. The other door was open, Maggie felt the chill of outer air like a fine spray over her cheek and shoulder. Of course, a rear exit would be an elementary precaution, and simple here in a labyrinth of castle cellars. They were all slipping away like flickering ghosts, the taciturn man who had cleaned the gun, the two big, raw-boned Austrians, the slender young one in the raincoat, the distraught sentry, all vanishing, all receding into tiny, rapid footfalls swallowed up by the rock.

Give him this at least, Robin was the last to go. He saw all his men away before he extracted the key from the rear door by which they had withdrawn, and passed through it in his turn, closing it briskly after him. His foot, as he crossed the room, stepped in the slowly-gathering rivulet of blood that seeped along between the stones. Maggie heard the key turn in the lock, and then his long, light steps receding rapidly.

It was very quiet in the wine cellar for a few blank moments, during which she drifted towards collapse, and dragged herself back desperately to press her hand against the hole in Francis's shoulder, where the blood pumped steadily out of him, sending thin, bright-red jets welling between her fingers. She hardly noticed when the new noises began, the shots that broke the lock of the outer door, the rush of feet advancing. Only when the battering at the nearer door began did she realise that the police were through one obstacle, and divided from her now only by that last barrier. She laid Francis down out of her arms gently, and went stumbling across the room to drag back the bolts. There were voices calling out to her from the other side, offering and demanding reassurance. She was almost too tired to understand or answer, but if she did not, Francis would die. She knew nothing about first-aid, but she knew arterial bleeding when she saw it.

"They've gone . . . another entrance somewhere . . ." Every word required an effort like shouldering the world. "He took the keys away . . ."

"Miss Tressider, are you all right?" That was an English voice, not just someone local speaking English. It made its way to the centres of energy in her exhausted mind, and she drew reviving breath. "Yes, I'm all right, but Francis . . . he's badly hurt . . . shot . . . Hurry, I'm afraid he'll bleed to death . . ."

"We're coming. We'll get through to you as fast as we can. Maggie . . . is he well away from the door? We may have to shoot a way through."

"Yes, near the other end of the room . . . ten yards . . . to your left . . ."

"Stay there with him, and keep down. Maggie . . . Maggie, can you hear me? *Where is he hit?*" George Felse was on one knee with his mouth as near to the keyhole as he could get it, yelling through to her over the probing and grating and cursing of an experienced professional struggling with the lock.

"In the left shoulder . . . an artery, I think . . . he's bleeding terribly . . ."

"Do you know where the pressure point is in the shoulder?" He told her in the fewest words possible how to locate and compress the subclavian artery. "You'll have to keep pressing . . . you'll tire . . ."

"I won't tire." No, not when she knew what to do. Her voice called back to him this time from farther away, she was already on her knees, raising Francis in her arms against the wall to strip away collar and shirt from his neck and feel for the pump that was emptying him of blood before her eyes. *But hurry . . .!*

"Good girl, we'll be through soon to help you . . ."

But the door was the door of a fortress.

*

From the moment that they found the Mercedes, tucked away in a hollow coppice on the Bregenz side of the castle hill, Oberkofler had taken no chances. He had a cordon of armed men strung round the hill on every side, methodically narrowing their circle as they converged on the unimpressive and unlovely ruins. Those on the Scheidenau side had neither seen nor heard anything of note since the discovery of the car, and were still merely carrying out their orders with proper attention, and no immediate expectation of incident, when their colleagues from the Bregenz side were already below the flagstones of the unkempt courtyard and battering at the first locked door. Their turn, however, came some minutes later.

The snaggle-toothed outline of what had once been a bastion, now reduced to a ragged stone wall no more than six feet high at any point, and overgrown with grass and weeds, reared from the smooth dark side of the hill ahead of them. And out of it, vaulting the wall at a low place, burst suddenly the figure of a man, running head-down for the gully of trees below. After him surged another, and another.

Gladly the police closed in. The first shout of challenge caused the foremost fugitive to swerve away towards the lake, where willing hands gathered him in without resistance, and the later ones to balk, break in various directions, and open fire. The police returned the fire, picked off the enemy singly and undamaged where they could, and shot to bring them down where they must. Five in all, but the fifth was no more than poised on the wall when the volley of shots broke out. He was notably quick and resolute in making up his mind. The bullet he put through the left upper arm of the nearest policeman was meant to do worse than wound, if the marksman's stance had not been so unstable. The policeman, firing back almost in the same instant, saw his opponent fall backward into the rubble and undergrowth inside the wall. But whether because he was hit or merely because he lost his balance no one was then clear.

By the time they had the other four secured, and came to look for the fifth, he had disappeared, though everyone was sure he had not emerged again anywhere round the perimeter. He had gone back, presumably, by the same way all five had come.

In the rank growth of early autumn it took them some time to find the broken place in the flooring within, and the steps leading down to the new, strong, locked door beneath.

*

He lay for a moment with the key still in his hand, feeling the waves of faintness approach and recede, and the slow drain of his blood seeping out of him. Here he could scarcely hear the shots from outside, and had no idea how long the skirmish continued; but he knew that they were all lost, every man of them. And he as certainly lost as they, though to another victor. All round the hill, waiting for them, the law. Down here in the rock, waiting for him . . .

How could it have happened, so unexpectedly and so finally?

Suddenly there were no continents left outside Europe, and Europe was crumbling away under his feet. All that carefully constructed kingdom, so firmly established, so long immune, wiped out in a night.

And all because of *her*. *She* had done this to him.

He did not know where the bullet in him had lodged, but he knew it was somewhere high in his chest, probably in the lungs. Bright red blood running out of his mouth, staining his hand, and the world sliding irrevocably away from him, and all at once this budding, proliferating pain where no pain had been, filling and overfilling him to the lips until he overflowed in blood.

He had always lived for his own advantage, pleasure and amusement, and in their cause everyone else had been expendable; and now that all these came down so catastrophically into one last small but sweet indulgence, he might as well continue consistent to the end, and rate himself as expendable, too. In any case he was all but spent. He knew he had not much time left, but he had time at least to kill the woman who had destroyed him.

With the last of his strength he set out along the passage, to crawl the ninety or so yards that separated him from Maggie Tressider.

*

Maggie, stiff and cold on the flagged floor by the open grave, holding Francis on her breast with his head carefully inclined and her thumb wedged hard down into the hollow of his collar-bone, heard the key grate in the lock of the rear door, clumsily and for some seconds abortively. She turned her head as if in a dream, without belief, and watched the door swing open, and no one come in. Nothing was quite real any more, except Francis, and the necessity to keep her thumb rammed into his gaunt flesh, and the awful, spurting flow stemmed. She did not move, even when she looked down from the place where the arriving face should have been, down below the lock, down to the creature who lay sprawled black and red across the threshold, with nothing live or human about him but the round, greenish-gold eyes in the ruined face, bent inexorably on her, and the right hand that still clutched the gun.

She raised her voice, not out of panic, but to reach the ears stretched to receive it beyond the other door, where the lock-breaker had been working now for many minutes:

"He's coming back!"

Someone outside cursed terribly. The door shook. George Felse shouted: "For God's sake try the gun . . ."

"He's come for me," she called clearly and calmly. It was there in his face. She watched Robin, and cradled Francis, gently retaining the blood in him, never moving.

Outside the door they were going mad. The solid wood shook and trembled and creaked, but held firm, the first burst of gunfire, from something surely larger than a pistol, splintered the woodwork and scarred the stone wall, but still the lock resisted. Inside the cellar it seemed inordinately still and quiet. They were two separate worlds. Maggie excised from her consciousness the one that was useless to her, and sat still, only following with her eyes the struggles of the creature in the doorway.

The gold eyes never left her. His free left hand reached up laboriously, with the patience, she realised now, that belongs not to angels but to devils, until it got a hold on the latch of the door, and held fast. The right hand that held the gun, so carefully, so tenderly because it was the only treasure he had left, prised him doggedly up to his knees. He shifted the hand then with slow, drunken concentration to the door-frame, where it clung by the side and heel of the palm, frozen to the wood by the icy coldness of his will. Nothing else was now alive in him, except the deep, secret nerve that reacted only to hatred.

With infinite effort he had got one foot flattened to the floor, and with clinging hands and sweating agony he was levering himself upright. It was impossible. But for the burning determination he had to kill her as she had killed him, he would have fallen down long ago and stayed down, and died where he fell. Instead, inch by inch he drove himself upright, and even as she watched him, he took one lurching step away from the wall.

Gently and regretfully she laid down Francis out of her arms, on his face, that the wound might bleed less. Rising, she stepped over his body, and stood between him and their enemy. In this last encounter she had to meet Robin on equal terms. This whole affair had begun with the two of them, and with them it must end.

Neither of them heard the renewed grating of metal at the lock, the shattering gunshot, the impact of massed bodies against the barrier. There was no one left in the world but Maggie, erect and motionless in the centre of the cellar, and Robin Aylwin, propelling himself in dogged agony almost to within touch of her. The levelled gun, as heavy as the world, wavered upwards by inches towards her heart, sank irresistibly twice, and twice was recovered and forced onwards, towards her heart, level with her heart.

With abnormal clarity she saw the crooked finger on the trigger struggling to command the strength to contract, and put an end to her. For an age the muzzle quivered, leaned, sagged from her breast, reared again and shook again, straining and ravenous for her.

The flame went out abruptly. The gun and the hand that held it trembled and sank, in spite of all his almost disembodied fury, sank and reached for the flagstones, subsiding into the dark. He pitched forward at her feet, and lay still. The bright blood from his lips stained her white slipper. The hand with the gun was buried under him.

The lock gave, the police flooded into the room. They saw her standing like a statue in ice and blood, her face as white as the ground colour of her own housecoat, blood on her breast and sleeve, blood on her shoe, where her enemy lay prone as if in worship, his curled lips kissing her instep. George Felse put his arm round her, and she crumpled into it with a huge, hapless sigh, and he picked her up bodily and carried her away, out into the air and the clean night emptied of enemies.

Behind him others at least as expert as he converged upon Francis Killian, and took charge of him until the ambulance came to rush him into hospital at Bregenz, where they would pump into him pints of blood, and stop the loss of his own. But it wasn't a hospital this one needed. George thought, as he always thought when the world closed in, of Bunty. He made for the nearest car of the several that had somehow gathered, and commandeered it without scruple, police driver and all. On the journey back into Scheidenau he held Maggie in his arms like the daughter he and Bunty had never had, and promised her the world and Francis, too, and never stopped holding her until he gave her to Bunty at the Goldener Hirsch.

*

So it was not until half-way through the next day that he provisionally closed his own case. They had excavated the sitting tenant of the wine cellar by then, naked, almost a skeleton, young, male, the errand-boy who knew better how to run the business than did the managing director. Maggie would clear up the references later, but up to then Maggie was a limp, wondering convalescent just coming to life in Bunty's charge, living on bulletins from the hospital in Bregenz, and not yet fit to be questioned. What mattered about the young man from under the flagstones was that his more durable parts, notably the teeth, bore certain unique characteristics which were ultimately to identify him beyond doubt as Peter Bromwich, the art student of Comerbourne.

And that, combined with the capture of four of the international gang which had been plaguing this corner of Europe for so long, made the nocturnal siege of Scheidenau Castle a highly profitable operation. All the more so as three of the four showed signs of being willing to talk for their own sakes, and possibly to bring in, indirectly, at least half a dozen others from the shattered brotherhood.

Not to mention, of course, their lord and master, Robin Aylwin, sometime 'cellist of Freddy's Circus, listed by the hospital at Bregenz as "Dead on arrival."

CHAPTER XIV

"I QUITE UNDERSTAND," said Maggie, picking abstractedly at the keys of her piano and frowning at the music before her, "that he doesn't want to see me, after all that's happened. What did I ever do for him, except make use of him, involve him against his better judgment in . . . all that horror . . . and nearly kill him? I don't blame him if he never wants to see me again. I haven't any right to force myself on him. Are you *sure* he's all right?"

"Right as rain." Bunty stood by the window, looking out upon the placid surface of the lake, pale in a still midday, bright but sunless. It was the ninth day since Helmut's night carnival, and the clear, chill peace of autumn lay over Scheidenau. "They wouldn't be discharging him in two days' time if they weren't satisfied, especially after all the fuss and all the reporters. Six pints of blood they've got staked in Francis, they're not going to waste that, you may be sure."

"Bunty, I owe you so much, you and George. *Bunty, help me!*"

"Did I ever say," wondered Bunty, "that he didn't want to see you? I said he *said* he didn't want to see you. In fact, I rather gave him to believe that you were going home with George and me, to-morrow. So he's due to come out of care the next day on his own, just the way he claims he wants it. He's ordered a taxi already, to take him back to the Weisses Kreuz. Most of his things are still there. He'll stay overnight, and then arrange his exit. He'll think he's clear of the lot of us. *You, too!*"

"Bunty, couldn't you find out for me what time?"

"I know what time. The taxi's ordered for ten in the morning. *Maggie, are you absolutely sure you know what you want?*"

"Yes, quite sure. *Yes, quite sure!* Oh, Bunty, pray for me!"

"Both of us will be doing that, naturally. For both of you!"

*

"Your car is here," they told him, and made their good-byes with warmth and ceremony, for he had been their prize patient for ten days, and when were they likely to get such another sensation? He packed his few toilet things in the briefcase George Felse had brought in for him from Schei-denau, along with a newly-pressed suit and clean shirt and underclothes to replace the ruins they had stripped from him and burned on arrival. He went down the stairs beside a gay little chattering nurse, and picked up at the desk his wallet and papers, with a note left for him by George and Bunty, wishing him luck and hoping to see him at home in England. Yes, perhaps. Nice people! They had visited him several times in hospital, and kept him informed about Maggie. Nothing from Maggie herself, of course. Well, that had been his intention, hadn't it?

So that was that. She had respected his wish to be left alone, maybe she'd even been grateful to him for taking the issue out of her hands. Back into your proper orbit, Miss Tressider, and I'll skid back into mine. I'll see you, he thought, from the back of the circle occasionally, I'll hear you broadcast and be thankful for that, but that's all the rights I shall ever have or ever expect in you.

He stepped out through the door into the cool, autumnal air, and shivered. He felt light, empty and aimless. The world was a big place, but without savour. He looked along the kerb for his taxi; there was little point in hurrying any-where, but none in staying here.

There was only one car drawn up by the entrance, and that was not a taxi. It was an elderly Dodge of a creamy coffee-colour, with a girl sitting behind the wheel.

She didn't get out when she saw him, but she leaned across and opened the passenger door, and waited for him to get in. Her hair was braided into two great plaits and coiled

on top of her head, and all those subtle colours that met
and married in it matched the leaves of the oak tree as well
in autumn as in spring. She was pale but radiant; all the
lines of her face were easier and more at peace than he had
ever seen them before, and her gentian eyes were no longer
straining to see something remote and ominous that would
not stand still to be seen. On the contrary, they focused
very sharply and resolutely upon him.

"I paid your taximan and sent him away," she said.
"You don't mind, do you? I'll drive you back to Scheidenau."

There was nothing to be done but get in beside her. "I
thought you'd gone back to England," he said, leaning
rather gingerly to dispose of his briefcase on the back seat.

"No, not yet." She started the car, carefully because she
wasn't yet used to it, and drove slowly out into traffic,
winding her way towards the frontage of Lake Constance.
"I waited for you."

"That was kind, but you shouldn't have put off going on
my account."

"To be honest," she said, "I put it off on my own account. Did you really think I could go away and leave you
here alone, after all that's happened?"

"I don't see why not. You'd already done more than
enough for me. You knew I was being perfectly well looked
after, and making a good recovery. And you must be longing to get back and start work again. I see," he said, veering
resolutely away from the subject, "they found the Dodge in
time."

"At that mason's yard in Regenheim. And quite a lot of
contraband and stolen property, too, that nobody had time
to ditch. When they'd done with the car I asked if I could
take it over. I thought you'd be relieved to see it."

"It certainly wouldn't be much fun to have to replace it.
It was good of you to think of putting my mind at rest."

Everything was going to be deference, kindness and gratitude, she could see that, whatever stresses might be gnawing away underneath. She waited until they were out of the

town, winding their way along the upland road, and then settled to a gentle forty kilometres, and cast a long, measuring look at him along her shoulder.

"You drive very well," he said. "I've never seen you in action before."

"You'll have plenty of chance, I'm driving you back to Zurich when we go."

"Maggie . . . now look . . ."

"Well, naturally! With that shoulder *you* certainly shouldn't be driving long distances yet. Though of course we could stay in Scheidenau for a week or two longer, if you like. It might be the best plan, actually."

"Maggie, look, you shouldn't have done this. I can't let you . . ."

"You can't stop me," she said gently, and turned and smiled at him. She would have to be very careful of him, she could see, he was still easily shaken. She felt his body tighten and brace itself beside her, and saw his brows draw painfully together over clouded eyes.

"Oh, no!" he said, shaking his head with decision. "None of that! I know you now. Once you passed by an overture of love, as you thought, without noticing it until it was too late, and spent years of your life paying your substance away in requital of what you took to be a debt. Now you're so mortally afraid of repeating the error that you'll fall over backwards to avoid it. But not with me! I've got too much sense to let that happen, if you haven't. You don't love me, you just feel responsible for me. You owe me nothing, and I'll take nothing from you. Go home, girl, sing, be successful, be happy . . . you've got time even for that, now."

"That," she said patiently, "depends on you. That's what I'm trying to tell you." They were high among the meadows, the hills folding and unfolding before them in bleached green of pasture and blue-black of conifers. She pulled in to the wide grass verge and stopped the car, turning on him a face pale to incandescence with solemnity.

"Francis, I'm not making any mistake this time, and I won't let you, either. I've never loved anyone before, perhaps I couldn't because of him. But I love you now, and if you pass me by I shall have lost everything. Maybe you don't want me, and that I could accept, but I daren't let go of you until I know whether that's really why you want me to go away. If you don't love me, tell me so, and I'll leave you alone. But for pity's sake don't tell me you don't if you do, because that wouldn't be noble, it would be damned ignoble, and I should spend the rest of my life paying for it, as well as you. And if you do love me, then start getting used to my being here, because I'm always going to be here."

He opened his lips to answer her, and found she had left him nothing to say. Everything he could have produced by way of subterfuge she had anticipated, and now he could not lie to her, even if he'd thought for a moment he could have managed it successfully. How could he live with himself afterwards, if he ever began to suspect she had been right? To send her back to her own world and her own kind might have been almost bearable, as long as he could rest in the conviction that she would be happiest that way, which God knew any sane man would take for granted. But what if the unbelievable turned out to be true, and he was the one who was fooling himself, not she?

He had begun to shake and sweat, between crazy hope and craven fear; this sort of thing wasn't for him yet, he wasn't up to it. He dragged his gaze away from her face with an effort, pressing his fingers deep into his hollow cheeks to clamp the wrong words in until he could find the right ones and somehow get them out. There are hurdles not even love can take without a crashing fall; only the native obstinacy recent stresses had roused in her could make her attempt them, and when the stresses passed, and even the memory of them grew pale, she would regret ever assaying the leap. She was a reasonable being, she would listen. And this wouldn't be lying to her.

"Maggie," he began laboriously, "have you really thought what you're suggesting? You know who you are, and what you are, nobody knows it better. A world figure, and going to be even greater . . ."

"I could," she agreed very quietly, "given the right circumstances."

"And I'm the right circumstances? Wake up, girl, for God's sake! I don't have to go into details about myself, and I'm not going to. Don't pretend you can't evaluate well enough to get my number right."

"Better, perhaps," she said fiercely, "than you."

"All right, let it go. But you know very well what I mean. You belong in a world about which I know nothing, among people with whom I have nothing in common, except, perhaps, a liking for music, and that wouldn't get me far. It's a live, mobile, important world, with no room for hangers-on. You know what I'm talking about as well as I do. Do you think that would be an easy marriage?"

"All right," she said after a long pause, her eyes wide and watchful on his face, "I do know what you're talking about, and no, it won't be easy. Did you ever hear of a marriage that was? But this one will be more difficult than most, I know it. And fathoms deeper! I'm not glossing over anything. I don't know any of the answers, those we have to find as we go. I'm simply telling you that there isn't any alternative! Marriage may be difficult, but separation is impossible. After what we've been through together, after what we know about each other, what do you suppose the ordinary pinpricks can do to us? Do you think two people ever drew as near as we have, and managed to pull themselves apart again without bleeding to death?"

He didn't know whether she had reached that argument by a lucky inspiration or by serious thought, but as soon as she had said it he saw that it was irresistibly true, and thanked God for it, since resistance was becoming unendurable. For better or worse, they had grown together until separation would have been extreme mutilation, a death before death.

Whether she had convinced him, or whether he had surrendered only to his own awful longing to be convinced, however it happened, suddenly she was in his arms. They had, after all, no option but to make their own rules, having strayed so far out of range of any others. Maybe she could never have married anyone now for the ordinary, socially respected reasons. Maybe he would really turn out to be what she wanted, and what she would continue to want, life-long. Please God, he thought. And God help us both, because we're going to need it! But when he kissed her all his lingering forebodings vanished like the mists dissolving over Lake Constance, and there was no room left in him for anything but incredulous gratitude and joy.

After a while they disentangled themselves silently and solemnly, and drove on mute and dazed with achievement into Scheidenau.

APPENDIX

Text of Maggie Tressider's English Singing Version of
"WHERE THE SPLENDID TRUMPETS BLOW"

"Wo die schönen Trompeten blasen," from *Des Knaben Wunderhorn*: set by Mahler.

> *Who's that without there, who knocks at my door,*
> *Imploring so softly, so softly: Sleep no more!?*
>
> *Your love, your own true love is here,*
> *Rise up and let me in, my dear!*
> *And must I longer wait and mourn?*
> *I see the red of dawn return,*
> *The red of dawn, two stars so bright.*
> *O that I were with my delight,*
> *With mine own heart's beloved!*

The maiden arose and let him in.
Most welcome home, my more than kin,
Most welcome home, my own true love,
So long you've watched and waited.
She offered him her snow-white hand,
Far off there sang a nightingale.
The maid began to weep and wail.

O do not weep, love, do not pine,
Within the year you shall be mine.
Ere long you shall be one with me
As never bride on earth shall be,
No, none but you on earth, love!

Across the heath to war I fare,
The great green heath so broad and bare,
For there, where the splendid trumpets blare and
*   thunder,*
There is my house, my house the green turf under.